African Mythology

Gods, Heroes, Legends, Myths of Ancient Africa

Jim Barrow

Contents

Chapter 1
General Overview of African Mythology

Mythology

Mythology is basically the study of myths. A myth is a story that people believe is true since it is usually connected to the history of the people. According to Encyclopedia Britannica (1133), a myth is "a story handed down in oral form from our forefathers which explains reality, concepts, and beliefs and further serves as explanations of nature and events such as creations, the origin of things, history of a race or a people."

Abu Nuwas (ca 756-ca 814)

Abu Nuwas, also Abu Nowas or Abu Nu'as, was a Persian poet in the 8th century who became a trickster-hero in the region of East Africa where Arabic culture is most dominant such as Madagascar, Mauritius, Tanzania, and Zanzibar. Abu Nuwas al-Hasan was his full name, and he was born in al-Ahwaz, Persia – now known as Ahvaz, Iran. The kalifs, Harun al-Rashid and his son, al-Amin both favored him, and he was quite successful at the Baghdad court up till the day he died. In the golden age of Arabic literature, Abu Nuwas is recognized as one of the great poets whose verse is said to be creative and combines humor and irony. It was his sense of humor and the continual quest for pleasure that made him appear in over one hundred myths as a trickster and jester. He was one of the characters in The Thousand and One Nights, which is also known as the Arabian Nights' Entertainment, a collection of myths from India, Arabia, and Persia.

A story of how his ingenuity entertained his supporters goes thus: On a certain day, Abu Nuwas visited the sultan while weeping and informed the sultan that his wife passed away. The sultan then promised that another wife would be found for him; the sultan's wife (sultana) brought him a maiden, and both Abu Nuwas and the maiden decided to get married. The couple received a lot of gifts from the sultan and 1,000 pieces of gold. Abu Nuwas and his wife were too carefree with their spending that they spent all the money they had received from the sultan. While in that situation, Abu Nuwas came up with a strategy to get money. He visited the sultan to tell him that his new wife had passed, but he didn't possess the funds to entomb her; this made the sultan give him 200 pieces of gold.

His wife, on the other hand, went on to inform the sultana that her husband was dead and that she lacked the funds to entomb him, and the sultana gave her 200 pieces of gold. That evening, when the sultan and sultana met, she informed the sultan that Abu Nuwas was dead; the sultan argued, saying that it was Abu Nuwas' wife that died. To resolve the situation, a servant was sent to the house of Abu Nuwas to see who was actually dead.

On getting to the house, the servant saw Abu Nuwas' wife lying 'dead' as Abu Nuwas had made her lie down and covered her with a sheet to make it look like her corpse. Doubting the report, the sultana sent a second servant who this time saw the corpse of Abu Nuwas, who had laid down and covered himself with a sheet, feigning to be dead.

Determined to investigate, both the sultana and sultan went Abu Nuwas and saw the supposed corpses of the couple; the sultan then made a decree that he would give 1,000 pieces of gold to anybody who would be able to reveal exactly what had happened. Hearing this, Abu Nuwas got up and told the sultan to give him the money; this made the sultan and sultana break into laughter, seeing that they had been clearly deceived. The sultan then gave Abu Nuwas the money.

Abu Yazid (Abuyazidu) (d. 947)

Abu Yazid, also, Abu Yazidu is a mythical hero of the Berber people of Algeria, Morocco, and Tunisia. He was the leader of one of the Berber folks, the tribe of Zanata. He spread the Kharajide faith across North Africa after taking it up and converting the people of his tribe to the religion. Because of this, conflict arose between him and the Fatimid kalifs, who at that time were the rulers of North Africa. Abu Yazid subdued a lot of significant towns when the Fatimid kalif, Imam al-Qaim was in power (933–945); this made the kalif to escape, seeking sanctuary in Mehdiya, a city in Morocco where Abu Yazid came and laid siege in the year 945.

Although Abu Yazid did not succeed in conquering the city after laying the siege, Imam al-Qaim was killed while the siege lasted. al-Mansur, the son of the Imam, took over from him, and although Abu Yazid's rebellion was great, al-Mansur was able to quench it. Abu Yazid then had to retreat to Susa. While Abu Yazid was in Susa, al-Mansur launched another attack at him, forcing him to seek refuge in Morocco, although he did not stop revolting against al-Mansur. It was later at Fort Kutama that Abu Yazid was discomfited and wounded while in battle. He died a few moments later. In spite of their differences, Abu Yazid was highly respected by al-Mansur so much that after Abu Yazid died, his family was catered for by al-Mansur.

Aiwel Longar

The mythical hero that is thought of as the ancestor of the Bor people, Dinka, Sudan, is named Aiwel Longar. Stories talk about Aiwel Longar. Some of the stories are regarded as enfant terrible stories – that is, stories that are about people who were borne in a strange way and possessed superhuman abilities.

One myth that talks about the life of Aiwel goes thus: A woman who only had a daughter was weeping because she had no male child, and her husband had passed away. A river god felt sorry for her and, with his waters, got her pregnant. The child she gave birth to was born with a full set of teeth, which signified that he had supernatural powers, and the woman named him Aiwel.

Although still a child, Aiwel was able to walk and speak, and when the mother found out about it, he warned her not to reveal it to anybody; when she did, she dropped dead. Then, Aiwel departed to live with the river god, who was his father until he grew up, after which he came back to the village where he was born with an ox having every last color on its skin. He came to be known by the name of his ox – Aiwel Longar after he had returned; he then took the herd of cattle that belonged to his mother's husband.

A time came when there were famine and drought in the land; the cattle belonging to the other villagers started to grow thin and eventually began to die. Aiwel's cattle, however, remained healthy and fat. Curious, a few young men decided to spy on him to uncover what was behind the health of his cattle and discovered that whenever Aiwel touched the ground, grass and water came up.

The young men described what they witnessed; all of them dropped dead. Aiwel then told the villagers that they had to leave the village in order to get away from the famine, offering to take them to a place that had many supplies to sustain them, but the villagers turned him down and went their own way.

When the people attempted to travel across a river, Aiwel started throwing spears at them, but one man was able to get close enough to hold Aiwel down until he could not move. Then, Aiwel permitted the people to get across, gave them his spears, and told them that he would depart and never return except when they needed his help.

Another version of this myth says that an old woman whose only child was a girl survived by catching fish in the river. A day came when she a certain creature in the river swashed water on her, and she became pregnant, but she did not give birth until after eight years – she gave the boy the name Aiwel; because the woman was well past the age of childbirth, the daughter refused to accept Aiwel as a brother.

Therefore, Aiwel began to live as a castaway who survived by keeping the cattle of the chief. The chief by the name of Fadol gave him a cow that became pregnant and gave birth to a yellow calf and eventually grew and became a spotted bull. This is why Aiwel came to be known as Aiwel-Longar. When a time of famine and drought came, every cattle in the land started getting thin and were dying except for the cattle of Fadol, which were being taken care of by Aiwel.

One day, Fadol followed Aiwel without his notice and saw that Aiwel hit the ground, and water and grass came out of it. Immediately Aiwel saw him, Fadol dropped dead, but Aiwel touched him and brought him back to life. The two of them went back to the village, and Fadol gifted Aiwel with several cattle and two beautiful women to become his wives. After Fadol passed, Aiwel became the chief, and his spear symbolized his power and divinity. Today, the priests of the clan of spear masters are said to have descended from him; the priests are the intermediaries between the gods and the people, and they are known to have killed the sacrificial oxen with spears.

Akoma Mba

Akoma Mba is of Fang origin, Cameroon, Equatorial Guinea, and Gabon. He was a Fang epos hero whose story showed that his behavior was not considered normal. As a child, he demonstrated his distinctness amongst other unique children who had supernatural powers. However, his behavior could no longer be predicted, and he eventually became a cause of pain to his family. Later in life, he became a warrior that was widely known who had a lot of conquests with various people, and in the end, he became king over the Ekang people.

Antar (ca. 525–615)

Antar, also Antara or Antarah, is a myth of the Bedouin people of Algeria, Libya, Morocco, and Western Sahara. Antar was a famous hero, poet, and a warrior who was born as a slave but then rose to become a headman. His full name was Antarah ibn Shaddad al-Absi, and because of his great acts, several legends were written and told about him in the Arabic epos known as Sirat Antar, meaning Romance of Antar.

He was wealthy, magnanimous, benevolent, and brave – a perfect representation of what a Bedouin chief should be. He wasn't born into leadership; instead, he achieved it through his strong sense of character and herculean spirit; he was a defender of people who were weak (suffering) and was very famous because of his bravery and valor. Legend has it that Anatar's mother was an Ethiopian slave, and Shaddad, the chief of the tribe of Abs was his father; but he was treated like a slave because he was not acknowledged as the chief's son. When he became 15 years old, he demonstrated his abilities as a warrior, and as a reward, the Shaddad granted him his freedom. Antar later became the chief of his tribe, and he was celebrated as a poet of his generation just as he is by modern-day critics. Despite not being a Muslim, one of the poems he wrote was awarded the highest honor that an Islamic writer could have, and it is exhibited at the entrée of the temple at Mecca.

As the epic, Sirat Antar narrates, Antar did not know that his father was the headman. He fell in love with his cousin Ibla (or Abla) and kept writing her love poems; annoyed by this, Malik, her father, and Antar's uncle consulted with Shaddad (the chief) and planned to have Antar killed. The reason they changed their plans was that they witnessed Antar put down a lion with bare hands.

When Antar found out that the chief was his father, he requested to be acknowledged as the chief's son, but the chief beat him up and threw him out. Antar then went on a quest, which is usually embarked on by epic heroes. Legend claims that he fought the king of Ethiopia and that Algeria and Morocco was part of his conquests. He also struggled and survived spirits and other spiritual forces as his quest took him outside North Africa unto Iraq, Iran, Syria, and Rome.

He had a lot of wealth during his return and didn't relent on his pursuit to marry Ibla despite how much her family resisted him. He went as far as killing a rival before her family finally gave up, and he took her to him home in a palanquin.

Bayajida

Bayajida is a fabled hero of the Hausa people of Niger and Nigeria. There are some stories of history that say he was the son of the king of Baghdad. Bayajida's Arabic name was Abuyazidu; hence, the claim that through Bayajida, the Hausas descended originally from the Arabs. Abuyazidu had a great army under his command, and after fighting a great battle against foes that launched an attack against Baghdad, he and his army roamed their way into Bornu in the northern part of Nigeria. On reaching Bornu, he and the sultan became allies, and together, they fought against any enemy that threatened Bornu territory. The people of Bornu gave him the name Bayajida, and he soon married Magira, the daughter of the sultan.

Bayajida grew popular, and he had a lot of wealth and power. This made the sultan jealous of him, and he tried to kill him. Magira found out about her father's plot and warned her husband, and both she and her husband escaped together. When they got to Garum Gabas, Magira discovered that she was pregnant, so Bayajida left her there and continued to travel until he got to a town known as Daura, which was under the rulership of a woman called Daurama.

An old woman let him take refuge in her house, and when he asked her for some water, she said that she didn't have any. The town only had one well from which to draw water, but a great snake lived inside the well, and the only way the villagers could draw water was if they all gathered together into a group of people that were strong enough to hold back the snake.

The woman's story didn't faze Bayajida as he took a bucket and went to the well and started to draw water. While drawing out the bucket, the snake clutched to the rope that it was tied to the bucket. With one of his hands, Bayajida grabbed the head of the snake and chopped it off. He dropped the body of the snake by the side of the well, but he took its head, put it in his bag, and headed back to the woman's house.

The following morning, the people saw the body of the snake lying dead around the well and took the news to their queen. The queen then made a decree that half her town will be given to the person who killed the snake. Many people claimed that they were the ones who had killed the snake, but none of them were able to provide proof (the snake's head). The woman who had been housing Bayajida went to the queen and told her about him and all that had happened, and then, the queen called for him.

When he got there, he showed her the head of the snake, and the queen proceeded to give him half of her town, but he declined. He insisted that she married him. The queen agreed, and they lived happily for a long time and had a son named Bawo. When they both died, Bawo ruled Daura in their stead; he had six sons, and they founded and ruled six of the seven Hausa states. The seventh Hausa state was founded by Bayajida's son from his first wife, Magira.

Ditaolane

Ditaolane, also Lituolone, is a diviner of the Sotho people residing in Lesotho. He is a mythical hero who had spiritual powers, and the story of his birth was strange. When Ditaolane was to be born, a fearful creature known as Kammapa was at the verge of devouring every human being. The only woman alive was the mother of Ditaolane, who was hiding at the time.

After Ditaolane was born, there were charms of divination about his neck. This was why his mother named him Ditaolane, meaning Diviner. Within the short period of time that his mother spent in gathering straw to make him a bed, Ditaolane had already grown to be an adult and was able to speak as though he was a sage. Noticing that the world was empty, he asked his mother why it was so, and she told him of Kammapa. So, taking a knife, Ditaolane went looking for the beast, and when he found Kammapa, he was swallowed whole though unharmed.

From the inside of the beast, Ditaolane used his knife to cut its intestines, and Kammapa died; then, Ditaolane cut open the beast's body from the inside so he could come out. Everyone who had been consumed before also came out with Ditaolane. Instead of thanking him, the people were afraid of him and even planned to have him killed, but because of his divination skills, he knew of their plot in advance, and the plan of the people failed.

He was being chased by his foes one day when he turned himself into a stone; one of the people chasing him became frustrated that they could not find him and picked up the stone and plunged it across a river. Ditaolane transformed back into himself and then continued his journey. A different version says that time came where he became weary of running to save himself, and he eventually surrendered to the people chasing him, and they killed him. After his death, his heart turned into a bird and flew out of his body.

Ebele

Ebele is a mythical hunter in the myths of the Igbo people of Nigeria. The Igbos think of Ebele as their ancestor even though there was no one that knew exactly where he came from. It is said that he just came out of nowhere and decided to reside in Ohanko (a town). During the intervening period, Ohanko happened to be at war with two other different towns towards the south, and so many people lost their lives in the process because while the war went on, the armies were fighting with spears and arrows that had been poisoned.

Ebele, on the other hand, had a firelock rifle, and with it, he went to fight for the Ohanko people, and most of their enemies died from his gunfire. Also, among the enemies were people who never came across a gun before. They were unaware of its capabilities and seeing things as though their brothers died because the weapon was powered by magic, they ran away in panic.

Ebele was heralded as the savior of the town of Ohanko, and the people made him a high occupant of their town. A couple of years after, Ebele provided a solution to a dispute that arose among two groups in the town, suggesting that one of the groups had to leave the town. After settling the dispute, he was made the chief of the town.

Funzi (Mfunzi) Fjort, Republic of Congo

Funzi or Mfuzi is a myth about a blacksmith of the Fjort people of Congo. His story shows that after the river god gave the Fjort people fire, Funzi was the one that taught them how to work using iron and copper. The Fjort people also acknowledge Funzi as the one who created lightning in that while he hit his hammer on his anvil, sparks came forth from it.

Chapter 2
Differences between areas and cultures inside Africa (ex. immigration, slave trade, colonialism, etc.)

Egypt

Egypt is a country in the Northeastern part of Africa, originally known as the United Arab Republic. The official language in the country is Arabic since the 7th century; *Masri* is the Egyptian Arabic dialect of the people.

Egypt is at the center of the foundation of African history. Proof of ancient civilization in Egypt (Egyptian empire) has been found to be in existence between 2600 to 30 BC.

Slave trade

People from the Oases, as well as Upper Egypt, were the main Slave traders in Egypt. Other major slave traders were the Bedouin people and villagers from Buhayra province. The traders were divided into groups of black slave traders and white slave traders, and they had an association. The greatest slave depot and front for the slave trade was Cairo. There was a yearly event for the trading of slaves called the mawlid of Ṭanṭā.

Colonization

French Domination of Egypt (1798–1882)

France was discovered to have invaded Egypt between the 17th and 18th centuries; however, the reason France finally landed in Egypt in the year 1798 under the leadership of Napoleon was that France was at war with Britain. Upon taking control, Napoleon did a lot to show that he supported Islam so as to gain the Egyptians' goodwill. During that time, animosity for foreign leadership grew among the Egyptians, and using barrage fire, they launched an unanticipated attack on the French.

Not long after, Napoleon faced defeat at the hands of Ottoman Syria when he tried to take control of Acre. This made him depart from Egypt, sneaking past the British fleet on the 22nd of August. The next French general in chief, Jean-Baptiste Kléber tried to take control of Egypt again. The Ottomans did the same; however, the French defeated them at Heliopolis. Soon after, Kléber was assassinated by a Syrian on the 14th of June.

The next person to take power was 'Abd Allāh Jacques Menou, and during his time (1801), Egypt was being invaded by the British forces from Abu Qīr, the Ottomans from Syria, and British Indian forces from Qusayr; French military surrendered in June at Cairo, and Menou surrendered in September at Alexandria. The British then established Dual Control over Egypt to rule besides khedives.

European Intervention

Egyptians took control of their country, and in the years 1805 to 1879, there were a lot of administrative changes; it was in 1879 that the Europeans began to rule over Egypt. Although Europe was in power, they ruled with apprehension.

British Domination (1882–1956)

Development in Egypt really kicked in when the British took authority over Egypt. The British government was liberal and reluctant because it seemed that establishing a formal political authority would result in a revolt from the sultan and other European powers. Though the British had to secure their interests, and that called for the presence of the military.

British protectorate over Egypt did not last because of the Unilateral Declaration of Egyptian Independence on the 28th of February 1992. A little later, Sultan Fuad declared himself King of Egypt even though the brits still occupied Egypt. Brits began to send forces to defend the Suez Canal following the Anglo-Egyptian treaty of 1936 as well as train Egypt's Army. In 1956, a coup d'état forced the brits to pull back their forces, and in the same year, Britain warred against Egypt over domination of the Suez Canal, but they lost.

Immigration

The first immigrants into Egypt were the Turkish, who departed from Central Asia. They arrived in a country that was home to one of the earliest civilizations of the world and who also contributed a great deal to the history of Islam due to their understanding of administration, military control, and very active culture. As a result of the occupancy of the Turks in Egypt, the Tulunid dynasty featured a series of Egyptian leaders who were either originally Turks or they were brought up in accordance with the norms of Turkish culture and state.

Although there are no records of any historical immigration into Egypt by the Turkish, a lot of Turks arrived at and occupied lands in the country. There are those who took place as their new home while others stayed for a period of time, and then they departed. Among the Egyptian immigrants from Turkey, some came to search for riches and better conditions of living while some came for official purposes, and others for the purpose of studying.

When the Turks were on the verge of losing the Ottoman Empire to Europe, its army arrived in Egypt under the leadership of Muhammad Ali' Pasha, and Muhammad Ali' took over the leadership of Egypt in 1805 up until 1952.

Legends

Legend of Creation

Heka is a force that existed before creation, which empowered the gods and is responsible for every aspect of life. Atum (Ptah) was a god that rose up and then gave birth to Shu (god of air), who gave the principles of life to the early world, and Tefnut (goddess of moisture), who contributed to the principles of order. Tears from Atum's 'All seeing eye' also birthed men and women. Shu and Tefnut gave birth to Geb (earth) and Nut (sky). Geb and Nut birthed Osiris, Isis, Set, Nephthys, and Horus.

Osiris emphasized *ma'at* (harmony) while ruling the world with his sister/wife, Isis but Set envied his power and glory. Set cut Osiris in 42 pieces and scattered the parts all over Egypt. Isis was in despair at Osiris's death and with the loss of his body, and immediately, she and Nephthys set out to find the parts. Upon finding a body part, they built a shrine to shield it from Set, and this gave birth to the 42 Egyptian provinces. When they gathered all the parts, Isis assembled Osiris and mated with him to give birth to Horus, after which Osiris went to the underworld, where he became the ruler of the dead. When Horus, Osiris's son, grew up, he challenged his uncle Set to battle, and Set was defeated.

Egyptians believe that after death, a person's soul appears before the Hall of Truth before Osiris for judgment. The white feather of ma'at is weighed against the person's heart; if the heart is lighter, it is allowed passage into the Field of Reeds (eternal bliss), if the heart is heavier, the soul is consumed by Ammut (gobbler) and ceases to exist.

Legend of Apophis

Another legend is that of Apophis, an evil creature resembling a dragon skull on the horizon and every evening. When the sun passes through the underworld, Apophis attempted to stop it. A clear sky meant the sun passed easily. A blood-red sun indicated a battle between good and evil, which left the sun victorious and meant new dawn.

Nigeria

Nigeria, officially known as the Federal Republic of Nigeria, is located in West Africa, having 36 states, and is home to ancient and indigenous pre-colonial states and kingdoms.

Slave trade

When the transatlantic slave trade commenced, slaves were supplied from the southeastern part of Nigeria to European slave traders by traditional slave traders. Despite the official ban placed on the slave trade by the British administration in the middle of the 1800s, it still continued silently up until the 1930s and was finally put to an end in the 1940s.

About 3000 people were taken as slaves from West Africa every year before the year 1650, and in the final quarter of that century, the number of slaves that left West Africa was 20,000 a year. Slave trade was worse between the years 1700 and 1850 – in those years, an average of about 76,000 people were taken from Africa between 1783 and 1792. When it first started, the trading of slaves was usually done in West Central Africa, now known as the Congo. The front for the sale of slaves moved to the Bight of Benin in the 1700s, and it came to be called the Slave Coast. The major ports on the coast for transporting slaves abroad were Ouidah (which is now a part of Benin) and Lagos. In Lagos alone, the number of slaves that were bought was about 2,000 between the years 1790 and 1807, although mostly by the British, but later, the Portuguese took over and started buying. In 1740, the main slave traffickers in the Bight of Biafra were the British – the ports in the Bight of Biafra include Old Calabar (Akwa Akpa), Bonny, and New Calabar. In 1767, the British made it easy for dozens of people to be murdered at Calabar after they had invited those people to their ships – the brits did this apparently to settle a local quarrel.

In the year 1807, the Slave Trade Act was enacted by the Parliament of the United Kingdom, which barred the British from partaking in the slave trade. When Britain ceased from partaking in the slave trade, it constituted a major decrease in the transportation of slaves to North, South, and Central America, and this decrease in the slave trade was what led to the collapse of the Edo Empire because it was the major slave-trading state. The French and the British bought more slaves from Edo ports than other European powers.

Lagos became one of the major slave ports in the late 1700s up to the 1850s. Most of the slave-trading done during that period was illegal, and as a result, there isn't much data to give the actual estimate of how many slaves were bought. However, the Trans-Atlantic Slave Voyage Database shows that 308,800 slaves were transported from Lagos across the Atlantic between the years 1776 and 1850. The French and the British were the most involved in the business of trading slaves until 1807 when the Spanish and Portuguese stepped in. Between the years 1826 and 1850, the Royal Navy of Britain started interfering with the trading of slaves from Lagos.

African and European historians continue to argue to this day whether the British colonized Nigeria because their motives were a benevolence toward putting a stop to slavery or because they just wanted to demonstrate their wealth and power. But the fact remains that slavery and its effects had already wiped out most of the Nigerian population to the point that there was chaos, which called for the enforcing of colonization.

Colonization

West Africa was under the rule of the British in the middle of the 19th century, and so, Great Britain colonized Nigeria. After the slave trade was prohibited, the brits occupied Lagos in 1861 and established the Oil River Protectorate in 1884.

Between 1886 and 1899, the majority of Nigeria was under the governorship of George Taubman Goldie of the Royal Niger Company. The control of the Protectorates of Northern and Southern Nigeria was taken over by the British government in 1900, and in 1906, the Lagos colony was merged with the Protectorate of Southern Nigeria.

The administration of the Protectorates was centrally under the Colonial Civil Service, which had Residents and District officers that were appointed over each region. Each region had a Native Administration led by District Heads and traditional rulers (Emirs in the north, and Obas in the south).

Sir Frederick Lord Lugard kept pushing for the entire Nigerian territory to be unified, and it wasn't till August 1911 that the Colonial Office asked him to lead the amalgamated colony. Lugard came back to Nigeria after his 6-year term as Governor of Hong Kong to supervise the merging of the northern and southern protectorates in 1912. On the 9th of May, 1913, he submitted an official proposal for both the northern and southern provinces to have separate administrations but remained under the control of the office of the Governor-General. The Colonial Office accepted most of Lugard's plans, but the idea of him being in control and making decisions without their consent didn't sit well with them.

Regardless, the northern and southern protectorates of Nigeria were officially unified and became one colony and protectorate under the control of the proconsul with the title 'Governor-General of Nigeria' in the year 1914. After uniting the northern and southern protectorates, the British employed the system of indirect rule to preside over the northern and southern regions.

The system of indirect rule where the structure of authority was focused on the emir did not bring about change in the north. While the emirs were very comfortable with their roles as dependable agents of indirect rule, the colonial masters did not do much; rather, they thought it best to leave things as they were, especially when it came to religion. Christian missionaries were not permitted in the north, and the little efforts made by the government towards educating the young were combined with Islamic institutes.

In the south, however, traditional rulers were a medium for the indirect rule in Edo and Yoruba lands except that the priestly functions of the rulers were weakened by Christianity and Western education. This called for dual loyalty; first, to the view of sacred rulership because of the symbolical value it held, and second, to the modern conception of law and governance. Because of the respect that was awarded to traditional rulership, the Oba of Benin, whose office lay with Edo religious belief, was allowed to assume sponsorship of a political movement of the Yorubas. While in the Eastern Region, the people did not accept the leadership of certain officials who were appointed and given 'warrants' – which led to the rise of the nomenclature known as 'warrant chiefs' – because they did not have any original traditional claims.

Uniting the Northern Nigerian Protectorate with the Southern Nigerian Protectorate entailed that there would be an informal relationship between three different subdivisions of regional governing bodies in Nigeria: the Northern, Eastern, and Western regions. Each of these regions had independent government roles and were ruled by a Lieutenant Governor who supervised almost all independent units whose economic interests coincided but had uncommon social and political interests. The colonial government was very careful not to do anything that was in violation of Islam so as to prevent any challenges that may step on traditional northern values and ultimately lead to opposition to British rule.

The process of governance with the system of an indirect rule meant that the local rulers had to interact with the colonial officials at all times, and the system was designed in such a way as to accommodate all the regions. For example, the rule of law was a decree that was signed by the emir and the Governor in the north, whereas, in the south, the Governor had to consult with the Legislative Council before making any legislative decisions. The recognized official language in the north was Hausa, and the colonial officials were required to know and understand it. The English language was the recognized language in the south. Differences in Regional administration was also recognized in the quality of the personnel appointed to every local region as well as the range of operations that they were capable of handling. The British staff in all three regions continued their operations in the same way as had been before the northern and southern protectorates were united.

F. Lugard submitted another proposal to the Colonial Office, which granted the Governor the liberty of not staying in the country on a full-time basis, and the proposal was accepted. As a result, for four months out of the year, Lord Lugard took stayed in London. However, a good number of the persons involved found it to be baffling, so they disapproved of it, and with time, the practice was terminated.

In the year 1916, F. Lugard created a body comprised of six traditional rulers that included the Sultan of Sokoto, Emir of Kano, and Oba of Benin to represent all the parts of the colony; the body was called the Nigerian Council. This council was a supposed means for members to express their opinions so as to give the Governor-General an idea of how to preside over the amalgamated state. However, during the meetings, F. Lugard only informed the traditional rulers about British policy, and all the leaders could do was to pay attention and concur.

Lugard kept trying to solidify the sovereignty of the British and ensuring local governance through traditional rulership. He disliked the fact that most of the educated and Westernized Nigerians were in the south, which is why he suggested that the country's capital be moved to Kaduna (the north) from Lagos, but the capital was never moved. F. Lugard passed down his authority as Governor-General to his successor in the year 1918 when his tenure ended.

Immigration

Immigrants into Nigeria were mostly from other African countries, especially West African nations. Statistics show that immigrants in Nigeria are from countries such as Ghana, Benin, Mali, Chad, and Niger. Most of the immigrants in Nigeria are Liberians.

Legends

Bayajida

This tale talks about a man that landed in Daura. He was a warrior by the name Bayajida. On reaching Daura, he wanted to drink water; he was told that a snake was living in the only well in the town, and the only way to draw water was when there were more people capable of holding down the snake. Bayajida went to the well alone, and while drawing water, the snake clung to the rope that was attached to the bucket for drawing the water. Seeing the snake, he caught it by the head with his left hand and used his sword to cut off the head. He placed it in his satchel and left.

When the queen of the town saw that the snake was dead, she promised half the town to the person who killed the snake. Many claimed to have killed the snake but were unable to provide proof. At this, Bayajida stepped up and showed the queen the snake's head. Queen Daurama offered him half the town, but he asked for her hand in marriage instead.

Shango

Shango (Sango) is the god of thunder and lightning, according to the Yorubas, who lives in the sky. He had three wives called *orisas*, meaning goddesses; Oya, who was the goddess of the river Niger, Oshun (Osun), who was the goddess of Osun river, and Obba (Oba), who was the goddess of the Oba river.

Shango is usually represented with two axes, which is the symbol of thunderbolt on either his head, his six eyes, and sometimes three heads. Sometimes he is represented with a ram, whose bellows sounds like thunder. His servants were Afefe (wind) and Oshumare (rainbow).

South Africa

South Africa is officially called the Republic of South Africa (RSA). It has three capital cities; Pretoria is the executive, Bloemfontein is the judicial, and Cape Town is the legislative. The largest city in South Africa is Johannesburg.

Slave trade

Jan van Riebeek, founder of the first Cape Colony in 1652, initially tried to negotiate for cattle and human labor. However, when the negotiations were dropped, the British then opted for slavery. A total of 250 slaves were first imported into South Africa in 1658, out of which only 170 made the journey. Slave traders from Ghana also sent 228 slaves to the Cape on the 6th of May 1658. From the year 1710, the population of adult slaves was three times more than the population of adult colonials.

The fleet of the VOC returning from Batavia and other eastern areas also carried slaves; slave trade was not legal in the Netherlands so the slaves could not be sent to Europe. As a result of this, the slaves were sold at better prices at the Cape than in the East Indies.

Colonization

Dutch Colonization

After the Cape sea route was discovered in the year 1652, Jan van Riebeeck set up a virtual station at the Cape of Good Hope, which is now known as the Cape Town, on behalf of the Dutch East India Company. Sometime later, the Cape of Good Hope turned into a place for an enormous population of vrijlieden or as they are also called, vrijburges meaning 'free citizens' – these are people who used to work for the Dutch East India Company and decided to stay in Dutch territories abroad after their contracts had been served. Dutch traders also brought a lot of slaves from Indonesia, Madagascar, and some areas of Eastern Africa into the Cape. The mixed-race communities that were formed came about through unions between vrijburgers, their slaves, and some indigenes. The Cape Coloureds is one such communities that was formed, and as a result, most of these people took up the Dutch language and Christianity.

When the Dutch tried to expand toward the east, it resulted in a lot of wars with the Xhosa tribe emerging from the southwest – these wars were later famed Xhosa Wars. Each side was competing for land near the Great Fish River upon which they could graze their cattle. Some vrijburgers who turned out to be independent farmers on the frontier were called Boers, and those among them who adopted quasi-nomadic modus vivendi were known as trekboers. The Boers created military reserves, which they called commandos and allied themselves with the Khoisan groups in order to force Xhosa raids back. The opposing sides continued to launch violent attacks on each other, and combined with this, there was a theft of farm animals for many decades.

British Colonization

Cape Town was taken over by the British between the years 1795 and 1803 so that the French First Republic that had invaded the 'Low Countries' wouldn't. Although the Cape fell back under Dutch rule under the Batavian Republic in 1803, in 1806, the British assumed control again. When the Napoleonic Wars ended, the Cape was formally given over to the British, and it became an essential part of the British Empire. The British started migrating to South Africa in 1818, and that was what brought about the coming of the 1820 settlers. The new settlers were allowed to settle for a number of reasons, which includes growing the European workforce as well as strengthening the regions around the frontier against any attacks from Xhosa.

The first twenty years of the 19th century featured a powerful Zulu people who, under their leader, Shaka kept expanding their territories. In the early 1820s, the wars that Shaka started indirectly caused the Mfecane – crushing – where about 2 million people lost their lives, which resulted in the desolation and depopulation of the inland plateau. The Matabele people (a branch of the Zulu) under the leadership of king Mzilikazi created a larger empire that comprised the highveld.

A lot of Dutch colonists left the Cape Colony in a sequence of migratory groups that were later known as Voortrekkers – meaning 'Pathfinders' or 'Pioneers' – in the 1800s because they didn't like being subservient to the Brits. The settlers journeyed to the future Natal, Free State, and Transvaal regions. The Boers became founders of the Boer Republics made up of the South African Republic (Gauteng, Limpopo, Mpumalanga, and the North West provinces), the Natalia Republic (KwaZulu-Natal), and the Orange Free State (Free State).

President Thomas François Burgers of the South African Republic (Transvaal) proclaimed war against Sekhukhune and the Pedi on the 16th of May 1876, but he was defeated on the 1st of August 1876. On the 16th of February 1877, a peace treaty was signed between them at Botshabel, and Paul Kruger took over after Burgers left because he failed to conquer Sekhukhune. The Brits, led by the secretary for native affairs of Natal, Theophilus Shepstone, then took over the South

African Republic (Transvaal) on the 12th of April 1877. The British also tried and failed to subdue Sekhukhune in 1878 and 1879 until November 1879 when Sir Garnet Wolseley attacked with 2,000 British soldiers, Boers, and 10,000 Swazis.

Immigration

Immigrants into South Africa from Europe arrived in the country between the middle and the latter part of the 17th century. They were people from the Netherlands, France, Great Britain, Germany, and Ireland. Later in the 20th century, more Europeans arrived in the country, mostly in search of better living conditions. In the middle of the 1970s, Portuguese departed from the colonies of Portugal in Southern Africa, such as Angola and Mozambique, after the colonies gained their independence and migrated to South Africa.

Legends

Captain Van Hunks

In the 18th century, according to legend, a sea captain, Jan Van Hunks retired to live on Table Mountain with his wife. Every day he went up the mountain to smoke his pipe and to see the view. One day he went up, and to his surprise, a man was already there; the man challenged him to a smoking contest, and Van Hunks won. The strange man was actually the devil who took Van Hunks with him because he lost.

The thick cloud hanging above Table Mountain today is believed to remain from the smoking contest.

Two Roads overcame the Hyena.

A hungry hyena saw a fork that split into two paths, each of which led to two goats caught in thickets. The Hyena couldn't decide between the two paths and decided to walk down the left path with its left leg and the right path with its right leg. The paths grew further, and the Hyena was eventually split into two halves.

This encourages people to choose a single path and be dedicated to it, or they will be stretched too thin.

Chapter 3
The story of ancient Africa at the dawn

Before the arrival of the Europeans in Africa, the human settlements in the continent were largely made up of primitive people. The major occupations were farming (growing crops and rearing of animals for food), hunting. The clothing at that time was usually a piece of cloth or leather that was worn in between the legs. The ends of which were inserted into a string that runs around the waist meant only to cover the genitals. Bracelets were worn on the wrists and arms to complete this mode of dressing. The men frequently carried bows and arrows, javelins, and axes with which they armed themselves.

Central Africa

Sao Civilization

Beginning from the 6th century BC and onward to the 16th century AD, Sao Civilization in Central Africa was very prosperous. South of the Lake Chad, by the Chari River, is a territory that is presently part of Cameroon, and Chad was where the Sao people lived. This civilization is the most formal civilization whose existence in the Cameroonian territory can't be in doubt since they left apparent hints regarding their existence.

There are many ethnic groups of southern Chad and northern Cameroon who say that they are descendants of the Sao civilization, and chiefly among these ethnic groups with such claims is the Sara people. Artifacts left behind by Sao people show that they were people who worked with their hands crafting bronze, copper, and iron items. Some of the findings gotten from this civilization are bronze sculptures, terracotta statues of humans and animals, coins, funeral urns, household utensils, jewelry, highly decorated pottery, and spears.

Kanem Empire

The Chad Basin was the center of the Kanem empire. Kanem Empire was the name given to this empire beginning in the 9th century AD down till 1893 when it became the independent kingdom of Bornu.

The empire had a large landmass covering the majority of Chad, some areas of present-day southern Libya, eastern Niger, northeastern Nigeria, northern Cameroon, some areas of the Central African Republic, and South Sudan. The rise of the Kanem Empire began in the 8th century in the north and east area of Lake Chad. Sometime in the 9th century AD, the Kanem Central Sudanic Empire was established at Njimi by the rovers whose language was Kanuri – their trading was centered on getting horses from North Africa and providing slaves in exchange. In the 11th century, the Islamic Sayfawa (Saifawa) dynasty was established by Humai (Hummay) ibn Salamna.

The dynasty of Sayfawa was in power for a period of over seven (7) centuries and was, therefore, one of the dynasties that have lasted longest in the history of human civilizations. Another major source of income for the empire was a tax imposed on local farms. The land of the empire was said to be large enough to contain a cavalry of 40,000, extending from Fezzan in the north and Sao state in the south. Islam was the main religion, and most of its citizens were frequent pilgrims to Mecca so much that Cairo had special hostels for Kanem pilgrims. The shrinking decline, and ultimate defeat of this great empire occurred in the 14th century when Bilala encroachers from the area around Lake Fitri attacked.

Borno Empire

In the 18th century, Bornu became a place where Islamic education was centered on. The empire once had a great army, but by failing to import more novel weapons, the army soon lost recognition, and the decline of Kamembu had started at that time. Drought and famine had been growing immensely as well as the internal rebellion in the pastoralist north, growth of Hausa power, and importation of small arms responsible for the extreme bloodshed weakened the *Mai's* (ruler) power. The last *Mai* was overthrown in 1841, and that brought the Sayfawa Dynasty to an end; in its place, the al-Kanemi Dynasty of the *Shehu* assumed rulership.

Shilluk Kingdom

The Shilluk Kingdom was established in the middle of the 15th century AD by Nyikang, its first monarch. South Sudan was where the Shilluk Kingdom was centered in the 15th century along with a long piece of land by the western bank of the White Nile, and at about 12° N from Lake No. Fashoda was the name of the town where the capital and royal residence of the kingdom were sited.

Baguirmi Kingdom

During the 16th and 17th centuries, the Baguirmi Kingdom stood as an independent state southeast of the Lake Chad, which is the present-day country of Chad. The kingdom came out toward the southeast of the Kanem-Bornu Empire. The first ruler of the kingdom was Mbang Birni Besse, and it was while he was still in power that the kingdom was subdued by Bornu and transformed into an affluent.

Wadai Empire

Wadai Kingdom was established by the Tunjur people to the east of Bornu in the 16th century, and in the 17th century, the center of the kingdom was positioned on Chad and the Central African Republic. It was also in the 17th century that the Maba people began its rebellion and established the Muslim dynasty. Originally, the Wadai Kingdom was a tributary of Bornu and Durfur; however, it became an independent kingdom and great opposition to the neighboring kingdoms.

Luba Empire

Around 1300 and 1400 AD, a member of the Balopwe clan by the name of Kongolo Mwamba (Nkongolo) united all the Luba people near Lake Kisale into one. He also established the Kongolo Dynasty that was eventually booted out by Kalala Ilunga. Ilunga then spread the kingdom out towards the west of Lake Kisale. Later on, a central political system of spiritual kings (*balopwe*) ruled in conjunction with a court council of head governors and sub-heads all the way to village heads. The political system of the Luba people later spread through Central Africa, southern Uganda, Rwanda, Burundi Malawi, Zambia, Zimbabwe, and western Congo. The *balopwe* were chosen by ancestral spirits, and so they had direct contact with the spirits and communicated with them. States that were merged into the political system and with their titles could be represented in court. The spiritual power of the *balopwe* was where their authorities lay. Not their military authority besides the army wasn't that large. The Luba was capable of collecting tribute, which they redistributed, as well as oversee regional trade. Many states branched out from the kingdom, and the founders of these states claimed that they are descendants of the Luba. The major empires that claimed to be descendants of the Luba are the Lunda Empire and Maravi empire; northern Zambia people (the Bemba and Basimba) are descendants of the Luba immigrants into Zambia in the 17th century.

Lunda Empire

A Luba from the Ilunga Tshibinda royal family got married to Rweej, the queen of Lunda, and unified all the people of Lunda in the year 1450. The kingdom was then expanded by *mulopwe* Luseeng. Further expansion of the Lunda Empire was carried out by Luseeng's son, Naweej, who later became known as the first emperor of the empire, and his title was *mwato yamvo* (*mwaant yaav*, *mwant yav*) meaning the Lord of Vipers. The empire continued with the political system of the Luba, and it integrated into the system the people it had subdued. A *cilool* or *kilolo* (royal adviser) and the tax collector were delegated to each subdued state by the *mwato yamvo*.

There are a lot of states who claim that they are descendants of Lunda. For instance, the Imbangala people of inland Angola claim that they are descended from the brother of Queen Rweej, Kinguri, who could not bear being under the rule of *mulopwe* Tshibunda. As such, kings of states who were founded by the brother of Queen Rweej were called *Kinguri*. The Luena (Lwena) and Lozi (Luyani) of Zambia claim that they are also Kinguri's descendants. In the 17th century, chief and warrior of Lunda by the name of Mwata Kazembe created in the valley of Luapula River, an eastern kingdom of the Lunda. Expansion of the Lunda to the west was what gave rise to claims by the Yaka and Pende that they are also descendants. Lunda empire was united into Central Africa with the coming of the western coast trade. The 19th century saw the last of the Lunda kingdom when the Chokwe invaded with guns as weapons.

Kingdom of Kongo

As in the 15th century AD, the Bakongo people, who were mostly farmers, were united together to form the Kingdom of Kongo under the leadership of their ruler named *manikongo,* whose dwelling place was the area of Pool Malebo, lower Congo River. The capital of the kingdom was M'banza-Kongo. Due to the fact that they were more organized than their neighbors, they subdued and turned their neighbors into tributaries. They possessed great metalwork skills as well as pottery and raffia cloth weaving. They encouraged trade between regions through a tribute system that was under the control of the *manikongo.* In the 16th century, the authority of the *manikongo* spanned through the Atlantic, which was west to Kwango River in the east. A *mani-mpembe* was delegated to all the territories under the kingdom.

Northeastern Africa (Horn of Africa)

Somalia

Islam was birthed directly across the Somalia Red Sea coast, and they traded with Arab Muslims. This was why merchants and sailors of Somalia that lived on the Arabian Peninsula were steadily influenced by the religion. As Muslim families migrated from the world of Islam to Somalia in the early Islamic centuries, followed by the conversion of the people of Somalia to the religion due to the aid of the Somalian Muslim scholars centuries after, the old city-states transformed into Islamic Mogadishu, Berbera, Zeila, Barawa and Merka who were a part of the ancestors of modern Somalians known as the Berber civilization. Mogadishu was later known as the City of

Islam, and it presided over the trading of gold in East Africa for many centuries.

Ethiopia

Zagwe Dynasty commanded authority over many areas of what is today known as Ethiopia and Eritrea between 1137 and 1270. 'Zagwe' is gotten from northern Ethiopia, precisely the Cushitic speaking Agaw. As of 1270 AD, Solomonic Dynasty took over the rulership of the Ethiopian Empire, and this continued for several centuries.

North Africa

Maghreb (Maghrib)

As of 711 AD, North Africa had been subdued by the Umayyad Caliphate, and so in the 10th century, most of the North African population were Muslims. As of 9th century AD, an end was put to the conquest of North Africa by Islam and its cultures. Although the Umayyads presided over the Caliphate, having their capital in Damascus, the Abbasids soon took over, and the capital was transferred to Baghdad. The people of Berber, however, who due to a rejection of foreign powers meddling in their dealings, adopted Shi'ite and Kharijite Islam, which was considered antagonistic to the Abbasids. A lot of Kharijite empires arose and were cut down within the 8th and 9th centuries while declaring independence from Baghdad. In the early 10th century, Syrian Shi'ite groups created the Fatimid Dynasty in Maghreb, conquering the whole of Maghreb in 950 AD and the whole of Egypt in 969 AD, thus cutting themselves off from Baghdad. In the year 1050, ¼ a million Arabs departed Egypt for Maghreb.

Sudan

People who are connected with the site of Ballana moved to Nubia from the southwest and created three kingdoms – Makuria, Nobadia, and Alodia – after Meroe was dismissed by Ezana of Aksum. Makuria stood across the 3rd Cataract toward the Dongola Reach, and its capital was located at Dongola. Nobadia was toward the north of the 3rd Cataract, and its capital was Faras; toward the south of the 3rd Cataract was Alodia with Soba as its capital. Later, Nobadia was annexed into Makuria.

Egypt

Rashidun Caliphate took over Byzantine Egypt in 642 AD. Normally, under the Fatimid Caliphate, there was prosperity in Egypt – there was an increase in the production of wheat, barley, flax, and cotton, and the dams and canals were fixed. Clothes made from linen and cotton became majorly produced by Egypt, which led to an increase in the country's trade in the Mediterranean and the Red Sea. Egypt even issued a gold currency by the name of Fatimid dinar, which came to be used for trading with foreign nations. Most of the nation's income was generated from taxes.

Egyptians, before the coming of Europeans, had a monarchy that they believed was divine.

Southern Africa

Great Zimbabwe and Mapungwe

The first state in Southern Africa was the Mapungubwe Kingdom, which came up in the 12th century CE and had its capital located at Mapungubwe. The kingdom attained wealth by directing the trade of ivory from the Limpopo Valley, copper from the mountains of northern Transvaal, and gold from the Zimbabwe Plateau located between Limpopo and Zambezi rivers.

Following the waning of the Kingdom of Mapungubwe arose Great Zimbabwe on the Zimbabwe Plateau. Great Zimbabwe turned out to be the first city in Southern Africa, and an empire was centered upon it. The people of Great Zimbabwe were builders, a skill that was passed down from Mapungubwe – they built the wall of the Great Enclosure. Great Zimbabwe was a major source of gold, and trade with Swahili Kilwa, and Sofala was what helped it to thrive.

Namibia

Most states in Southern African were already established as of 1500 AD. The Ovambo in northwestern Namibia were farmers by occupation while the Herero were herders. With the increase in the number of cattle, the Herero moved toward the south to central Namibia to get access to better land for grazing. The Ovambanderu expanded to Ghanzi in northwestern Botswana. The Nama people who raised sheep and spoke Khoi moved up north till they met with the Herero; the struggle for land led to conflict between them.

South Africa and Botswana

Sotho-Tswana

Sotho-Tswana states began to develop toward the south of the Limpopo River in 1000 CE. The power of the chief of these people was determined by how much cattle he had and the connection he had with the ancestors. The power residing within cattle numbers stood till around 1300 AD. Various people of these states were linked to the Indian Ocean through the Limpopo River.

Nguni Land

One great period of disorderliness in southern Africa was *Mfecane* meaning 'the crushing', which was initiated by northern Nguni kingdoms, which include Mthethwa, Ndwandwe, and Swaziland because resources were scarce and there was famine. After the death of Dingiswavo of Mthethwa, Shaka took over. Shaka was a member of the Zulu people, he established the Zulu Kingdom, and he used his powers to rule over the Ndwandwe and moved the Swazi up north; when Ndwandwe and Swazi scattered, it led to the dissemination of Mfecane. Shaka extended the kingdom so much that the kingdom had tributaries coming from deep in the south – the rivers of Tugela and Umzimkulu. Shaka was killed by his half-brother Dinganne in 1828.

Khoisan and Boers

People were integrated into the Bantu people like Sotho and Nguni when Bantu was expanded. However, that ended because of the winter rainfall in the region. Khoisan people had trade exchanges of products like cattle, sheep and hunted game with the Bantu people for copper, tobacco, and iron.

Southeast Africa

Swahili Coast

The interaction with Muslim Arab and Persian traders led to the development of the mixed Arab, Persian, and African Swahili city-states, and the Swahili culture that emanated from these interactions show influences of the Arabs and Islam that had not been experienced in Bantu culture. The Bantu people of earlier times that occupied the Southeast coast of modern-day Kenya and Tanzania, who came across settlers from Persia and Arabia, acknowledged the trading settlements of Azania, Menouthias, and Rhapta; this is what eventually led to the derivation of the name, Tanzania.

According to history, far up north as northern Kenya and deep down south as Ruvuma River in Mozambique are places you can find Swahili people.

Urewe

Urewe culture was widely spread through the region of Lake Victoria in the African Iron Age. Artifacts of the people of this culture can be found in the Kagera Region of Tanzania, the Kivu region of the Democratic Republic of Congo down to the Nyanza and the Western provinces of Kenya. The culture of the Urewe people goes far back as the 5th century up to the 6th century AD, and the culture's origin emanates from the Bantu expansion from Cameroon.

Madagascar and Merina

Settlers from Southeast Asia who speak Austronesian were the first to land in Madagascar before the 6th century AD, followed by the Bantu people from the East African mainland during the 6th or 7th century. Cultivation of rice and bananas was brought in by the Austronesian speakers, while cattle rearing and other forms of farming were brought in by the Bantu. Islam was introduced to Madagascar during the 14th century, and during the Middle Ages of East Africa, Madagascar was functioning as a port where Swahili seaport city-states like Sofala, Kilwa, Mombasa, and Zanzibar came in contact. Just past the 15th century, the emergence of kingdoms like the Sakalava

Kingdom, Tsitambala Kingdom, and Merina began, and during the 19th century, the whole of Madagascar was under Merina control.

Lake Plateau states and empires

Kitara and Bunyoro

In 1000 AD, a lot of states emerged on the Lake Plateau from amongst the Great Lakes of East Africa. These states were into the cultivation of bananas, herding cattle, and cultivating cereals. The Bunyoro Kingdom is one of these first states (a part of the Kitara Empire). It ruled the entire region of the Great Lakes. This was a society whose culture was Nyoro at its core.

Buganda

Kato Kimera founded the Kingdom of Bugunda in the 14th century AD. The kingdom was under the rulership of the *kabaka* and clan heads known as the *Bataka*. After a period of time, the powers of the *Bataka* were reduced by the *kabakas* as Bugunda aimed at achieving an empire with a central authority. In the 16th century, Bugunda was trying to expand its lands, but it was rivaled by Bunyoro. Bugunda later in the 1870s became a very rich nation-state under the rulership of the *kabaka* and the then existing *Lukiko* – council of ministers. Not too long after, Bunyoro was conquered by Bugunda.

Rwanda

The Rwanda Kingdom was established somewhere around the 17th century at the bottom part of the western rift, near Lake Kivu. The elite groups of the kingdom were made up of bucolic Tutsi (BaTutsi), including the king known as *mwami*. The other group known as the Hutu (BaHutu) were farmers, and although they spoke one language with the Tutsi, certain stringent social standards did not allow them to interact or even marry. As oral tradition espouses, *Mwami* Ruganzu II – Ruganzu Ndori founded the Kingdom of Rwanda between 1600 and 1624.

Burundi

The Kingdom of Burundi was founded by Tutsi chief Ntare Rushatsi and is located toward the south of the Kingdom of Rwanda. The bedrock upon which this kingdom was established includes cattle herding, cultivation by Hutu farmers, conquest, and politics.

Maravi

The Maravi people claim to have descended from Karonga (*kalonga*). They were the ones who linked Central Africa with Swahili Kilwa to the east coastal trade. The king of the Maravi people was called *karonga*. In the 17th century, the Maravi Kingdom had covered the area around Lake Malawi and the outskirts of the River Zambezi. *Karonga* Mzura tried to expand the kingdom; his death really impacted the empire, and it finally split in the 18th century.

West Africa

Sahelian empires and states

Ghana

As of the 8th century AD, the Ghana empire was founded by Dinge Cisse among the Soninke, and it became an established empire. The empire was made up of urban dwellers who were part of the empire's administrators and the rural farmers. Administrative power rested not only on urban dwellers whose religion was Islam, but also the *Ghana* (king) whose religious practice was traditional. There were two towns; the first was where the Muslim administrators, as well as the Berbers, lived, which had a pathway to the king's house paved with stone, while the other was the villages which were meant for rural dwellers that combined with larger societies who swore loyalty to the king. After subduing Aoudaghost, the empire converted to Islam, and by the 11th century, it began to wane.

Mali

Mali Empire was instituted in the 13th century AD following the defeat of the king of Sosso (southern Soninko), Soumaoro Kanté, by Sundiata (Lord Lion), who was the leader of Keita clan known as Mande (Mandingo) during the Battle of Kirina of the 12th century. After winning the war, Sundiata based the empire's capital at Niani. Despite their trading of salt and gold, a vital part of their economy was agriculture, and so was cattle, goat, sheep, and camel herding.

Songhai

Songhai people are the descendants of fishermen on the Middle Niger River with their capital based at Kukiya in the 9th century AD but was later moved to Gao around the 12th century. Songhai Empire was expanded to the north by Sonni Ali, and his move forced the Mossi closer toward the south of the Niger.

Songhai Empire was occupied by Morocco in 1951 under the rule of Ahmad al-Mansur of the Saadi Dynasty, and the aim was to possess the Sahel where gold could be mined. Djenne, Gao, and Timbuktu were captured by Morocco. However, they could occupy the entire Songhai region. In the 17th century, Songhai broke up into numerous states.

Sokoto Caliphate

The Fulani were always migrating, departing Mauritania, they formed settlements in Futa Tooro, Futa Djallon, and after some time, they were spread throughout West Africa. They converted to Islam in the 14th century CE, and they based themselves at Macina, southern Mali, by the 16th century. They declared jihads on non-Muslims in the 1670s, and many states were formed as a result of the jihad wars at Futa Tooro, Futa Djallon, Macina, Oualia, and Bundu. Among the states that were consequently formed was the Sokoto Caliphate, also called the Fulani Empire.

Forest empires and states

Akan kingdoms and the emergence of the Asante Empire

The language of the Akan people is Kwa. Many are of the opinion that people who speak Kwa originated from East/Central Africa prior to their settlement in the Sahel. The Akan Kingdom of Bonoman was established in the 12th century. When the mines of gold in present-day Mali began to dry, all the Akan states, including Bonoman, started to rise in the gold trading market. The Empire of Ashanti (Ashante) was heralded by Bonoman and other kingdoms Denkyira, Akyem, and

Akwamu. During the 17th century, the people of Akan inhabited the state known as Kwaaman, located towards the north of Lake Bosomtwe. Its major source of revenue was derived from the trade of gold and kola nuts and forest clearing for the planting of yams. Ashanti Empire formed defense alliances with other kingdoms and became a tributary to Denkyira, Adansi, and Akwamu. The Ashante Empire stood for many years until it was destroyed by the British in 1900.

Dahomey

The Kingdom of Dahomey was established during the early period of the 17th century following the departure of the Aja people from the Allada kingdom to the north, where they took root among the Fon. By declaring their powers, a couple of years after their settlement, they created the Dahomey Kingdom, and the capital was located at Agbome. Between 1645 and 1685, king Houegbadia pronounced that every land in the kingdom would be owned by the king and should be taxed; he also turned the kingdom into a centralized state.

Yoruba

Yorubas thought of themselves as the people who lived in a United Kingdom. In 1000 AD, the first Yoruba city-state was founded and named Ile-Ife. Yorubas were ruled by an *Oba* with the *iwarefa* (council of chiefs) as his advisors. A loose confederacy of Yoruba city-states was created in the 18th century with Ife as the capital under the rulership of the Oni of Ife. During the 16th century, the Oyo Empire came up.

The Oyo Empire had a governing council, and for every region that the empire acquired, a local administrator was appointed to preside over it. Some of the productions of the Yoruba people include cloth, ironware, pottery, which was traded in exchange for salt, leather, and horses.

Benin

The Benin Empire had already been constituted in at mid-15th century. The empire sought to expand its borders and rule politically from early times. It was ruled by the *Oba* – meaning king – Ewuare between 1450 and 1480 AD, who, after strengthening central power, went to war against the neighboring kingdoms for 30 years. Benin expanded to reach Dahomey in the west, the Niger Delta in the east through the west African coast toward the Yoruba lands in the north, when he died.

The *Oba* got advice from the *uzama*, which was a council of chiefs and families with great power and influence, and town chiefs of different societal groups. After a period of time, the power of the *uzama* was weakened when administrative personnel was appointed. Furthermore, women were allowed to assume positions of authority. The queen's mother, for example, the mother of the oba of the future, had enormous power and influence.

Niger Delta and Igbo

Niger Delta in Nigeria is made up of many city-states that had diverse governments and were guarded by the delta waterways and thick vegetation. The city-states of the Niger Delta could be compared to the Swahili in East Africa. Places like Bonny, Kalabari, and Warri had kings; some such as Brass were republics that had small senates, while those in Cross River and Old Calabar were under the rulership of *ekpe* society traders.

The Igbo people resided towards the east of the delta while Aniomas, towards the west of the River Niger. In the 9th century, the Nri kingdom came up with its ruler called *Eze* Nri. It was a political unit that was comprised of independent and sovereign villages that had their own territories and names and were recognized by the towns and villages. The villages employed the majority rule (democracy) – its men, and sometimes women were included in the procedures for decision-making.

Chapter 4
God's and goddesses from the African continent

God's

1. Abassi

Abassi (Abasi) is the name given to the supreme god and creator among the Anang, Efik people of Nigeria who lived in the sky. He had two aspects to him; Abassi Onyong meaning 'the god above' and Abassi Isong, which means 'the god below.' Abassi created the world as well as the primeval man and woman, but he didn't want any competition, so he didn't permit them to live on earth, but his wife Atai disagreed, and Abassi was then forced to permit the primeval human couple to live on earth with the conditions that they refrain from reproducing or farming. The couple later went against the conditions and began tilling the ground as well as having children; this made Atai send death into the world. As a result, the couple died, and discord rose amongst the children.

2. Abradi

Abradi is the name given to the supreme god and creator among the Ama, Nyimang people of Sudan who lives in the sky. He is known to have unlimited power, which comes directly from him. People call on him in times of famine, drought, and epidemic. Once the sky was so close to the earth, women had to bend to cook; an annoyed woman stabbed the sky with a stirring rod, and this made Abradi angry so that he moved the sky far away from the earth.

Usually, when a person died, Abradi brought the person back to life the next day. However, a rabbit went to the people and told them to bury the dead man, or else Abradi would destroy them, and the people did so out of fear. Upon finding out, Abradi then declared that death would from thence be permanent.

3. Adroa

Adroa is of Lugbara, Democratic Republic of Congo, Sudan, and Ugandan origin. It is the name given to the supreme god and creator of all things. He had two aspects to him, just like many of the African gods; Adroa and Adro. Adroa was the sky god. He surpassed every limit of experience and knowledge of humans, which is why he stayed in the sky, and he was conceived of as *onyiru*, which means 'good.' It is said that Adroa created the primeval man whose name was Gborogboro and a primeval woman whose name was Meme (they were twins). Meme became the mother to all the animals. She also gave birth to male and female twin children. The aboriginal sets of twin children were not exactly humans in that they possessed superhuman abilities and magical powers, and they could do all sorts of amazing things. However, after many coevals that featured the birth of male and female twin children, Jaki and Dribidu, known as the hero ancestors, were born; their sons are believed to be the ones who established the modern-day Lugbara clans.

Adro was the god of the earth who existed and lived with humans and had the same limits as humans did; he was conceived of as *onzi*, which means 'bad.' His children were known as the Adroanzi. Furthermore, Adro was identified with death, and to gain his favor, humans had to use their children as a sacrifice. However, eventually, rams became the object of sacrifice instead of children.

4. Abgé

Abgé is of Fon origin in Benin Republic. Among all the Fon gods or deities known as Vodun, Abgé is among the chief of the Sea gods, which is one of the four gods into which Vodun was split into. He is the third son that was born to the Creator, Mawu-Lisa. He had a female twin sister by the name of Naètè, who was also his wife. At the time Mawu-Lisa split the various kingdoms of the universe amongst her children, she gave the sea to Abgé and Naètè to inhabit, and the command of the waters was given to them.

5. Agé

Agè is also of Fon origin in Benin Republic. He is a member of the Fon gods or deities (Vodun). Specifically, he is the god of the hunt and the fourth son born to Mawu-Lisa, the Creator. At the time Mawu-Lisa split the kingdoms of the universe amongst her children, she put Agè in charge of every land that was unoccupied and placed him in command of all game animals and birds.

6. Agipie

Agipie is of Turkana, the origin of Kenya. It is the name given to a god who had two different aspects to him that were at war with each other. The one aspect of Agipie was that of a good-hearted sky god, while the other aspect was that of a dangerous earth god that was identified with lightning and drowning. At whatever time, the two gods shot lightning bolts toward the other when fighting against each other, the result was the occurrence of a thunderstorm.

7. Ajok

Ajok, also known as Adyok or Naijok, is of Lotuko origin in Sudan. This is the name given to the supreme god and creator who in himself had a nature of benevolence; however, humans were required to constantly pray to him as well as offer up sacrifices, just so his good-hearted nature will be maintained. The Lotuko people tell a story of how death originated – it is said that a quarrel between a husband and his wife was what made Ajok angry to the point that he made death a lasting situation.

When the child of the man and woman was deceased, the mother pleaded with Ajok to restore her child's life, and Ajok did exactly that; however, when the husband found that his child was brought back to life, the husband was so furious that he lambasted his wife and killed the child. What ensued between the couple caused Ajok to make a decree to never bring any human back to life again, and from that moment on, death became a lasting and irreversible situation.

8. kongoo

Akongo is the supreme god of the Ngombe people in the Democratic Republic of Congo. He is known to have a close relationship with a human in the beginning, and he guarded and protected them. But with time, humans were given to quarreling, and when the quarrel amongst them grew severe, Akongo had to leave them and exiled himself to live in the forest, and since then, he was no longer seen or heard from.

9. Amma

Amma is the name given to the creator (god) people of the Dogon people of Mali and Burkina Faso. Some versions of the creation account of the Dogon people depict Amma as a male, while in some others, Amma is a female. The world and everything that exists within it was created by Amma; the earth was created when a lump of clay was projected into the heavens by this god. The sun and the moon were created when he took two earthenware bowls and shaped them, wrapping the bowl meant to be the sun in red copper while he wrapped the bowl meant to be the moon in white copper or brass. He then broke a piece of the sun, shattered the piece he broke, and threw the bits into space to form the stars. Another version states that he took pieces of clay and plunged them into the heavens. To the people of Dogon, the universe stands at the center of a world axis pillar known as Amma's House Post. This post also bears the sky, which the Dogon people believe is the roof of Amma's house.

10. Arebati

Aberati, also known as Arebate, Baatsi, and Tore amongst the Efe and Mbuti people of the Democratic Republic of Congo, is the supreme god and creator and god of the sky, but is also identified with the moon. Out of the 10 populations of Pygmies, the Efe and Mbuti are two. Some other groups of Pygmies believe Khonvoum to be the supreme god and creator instead of Arebati. In some groups, Aberati and Tore are the same, while other groups consider Aberati as the moon god while they view Tore as a god of forests and the hunt.

It is believed that the universe was created by Aberati as well as the primeval man who he formed from clay with the help of the moon; after Aberati had finished making the body of the man, he covered the clay with skin so as to bring the man to life. In the beginning, death was non-existent. Aberati made humans young again when they had grown old, and when a certain woman died, he restored her life. Aberati requested that a frog move the woman's body; however, a toad made a demand that he wanted to be the one to move the body, and Aberati permitted him. The toad was to sit with the body of the woman at the edge of a pit (symbolizing a grave) with a warning that neither of them (toad or woman) was to fall into the pit as there would be consequences. The toad fumbled, bashing the body of the woman into the pit, and he fell in as well. Based on the warning Aberati gave, there was a consequence as humans were doomed to die from that moment on.

A different myth tells that the supreme god known as Baatsi in the Efe story and Tore in the Mbuti myth told humans that they were free to eat the fruit of any tree except *tahu* and strict obedience to this rule awarded them the opportunity to live in the sky with Baatsi. A certain woman who was pregnant wanted to eat the *tahu* fruit so bad that she asked her husband to pick some for her. Dismayed by their disobedience, Baatsi sent death as a punishment.

11. Arum

Arum is the name given to the supreme god and creator among the Uduk people of Ethiopia, who is believed to have made everything that exists. The myth says that a great tree known as the *birapinya* tree connected the heavens with the earth; it reached the sky although the sky was closer to the earth than it is today, and humans, as well as the people living in the sky, used this tree as a means of conveyance between the earth and the heavens. The tree was cut down by a woman who thought she had been wronged, and so the conveyance was put to an end; the distance between the sky and the earth increased. Before the tree was cut down by the woman, death was not a lasting situation, but after the tree was cut down, it became permanent.

12. Asis

Asis, also called Asista, is the name given to the supreme god who created the sun, moon, sky, and earth among the Kipsigis, Nandi people of Kenya. He is represented by the sun, and working through the sun, he created every creature of the earth from air, earth, and water. Next among his creation were the first four beings, which include a human, an elephant, a snake, and a cow. Despite being distant from humans, he provided them with all that was good and was the force underlying everything in the world. The spirits of the dead known as *oiik* were the mediators between humans and Asis, and whenever the balance of nature was disrupted by the humans, the *oiik* punished them.

13. Ataa Naa Nyongmo

Ataa Naa Nyongmo is the supreme god who created the world and everything that exists within it. He is usually identified with the sky. Ataa Naa Nyongmo was conceived of as a god that nurtures, which is typical of a cultural group that was into agriculture. He commanded rain, sunlight, and growth of crops. Whenever humans failed to properly perform their rites or went against his commands, he withheld the necessities of life from them as a punishment, or sometimes he caused the occurrence of destructive natural events like earthquakes.

14. Bumba

Bumba is the supreme god of the Bushongo people of the Democratic Republic of Congo. At the very beginning, there existed only water and darkness, and Bumba was alone. He had a stomachache and started to throw up; the first thing he spewed was the sun, and there was light, and the next thing he spewed was the moon and the stars. By vomiting again, Bumba brought out different animals, birds, and fish, and lastly, he chucked up humans. All the creatures he vomited were the foundation for other animals to be created; all the birds were created from a heron, lizards and other reptiles were created from a crocodile, all other insects were created from the beetle, and on it went. Bumba had three sons who completed the fashioning of the universe, and when all of it was done, it was given unto humans.

15. Chukwu

Chukwu, also known as Chi, is the supreme god and creator from whom all good came according to the Igbo people of Nigeria. He is also the head of all the gods of the Igbo people, and he had three aspects to him (a tercet); Chukwu, his foremost aspect means the great god; Chineke means the creative spirit, and Osebuluwa means the one who governs and directs everything. The sun was used to represent Chukwu. He commanded rainfall and the growth of plants. Just as is the case with a lot of African deities, Chukwu was originally living in the sky, and the sky was close to the earth so that humans could touch it. Because of the close proximity of the sky to the earth, a woman pounding her mortar with a pestle tended to hit the sky with the pestle, and when Chukwu requested that she should stop, she refused to listen, so he moved the sky far above the earth and was thus separated from his creations since that time.

When death came into the world in Igbo tradition, humans sent a dog to ask Chukwu to bring people who had died back to life; but a toad who caught the message and wanted to punish the people went ahead of the dog and told Chukwu that human didn't want to be restored to life after death. Chukwu agreed to this and was unable to change his mind even after the dog who had the accurate message arrived.

16. Deng

Deng or Denka (meaning) rain is a deity of rain and fecundity of the Dinka people of Sudan. He was the mediator that stood between humans and the supreme being, and sometimes he was either referred to as the son of God or as the son of the goddess Abuk. Deng and the supreme god Nhialic were close, and in some regions, they are seen as the same deity. A story of the origin of Deng includes myths that are nonconforming, telling stories of children who were born in an unconventional way and possessed supernatural abilities (powers).

A young lady who was pregnant appeared from the sky, and people welcomed with great esteem to the point that a house was built for her. When she finally put to bed, the child that was delivered to her had a full set of adult teeth (which was considered as a supernatural power), and his tears were blood. The woman declared that her young child would be the leader of the people, and upon her proclamation, there was a heavy downpour of rain, and that was how the child got his name (Deng), which means rain. Legend has it that Deng exercised authority over the people for years, and when he became old, he vanished in a storm.

17. Djakomba

Djakomba, also Djabi or Djakoba, is the supreme god and creator – the god of the sky with a voice of thunder and could strike people down with lightning – of the Bachwa people of the Democratic Republic of Congo. He is believed to be the creator of everything that exists, including the primordial human being (the Bachwa people) ergo the Bachwa people refer to themselves as the 'children of Djakomba.' The sky god provided humans with life and food for their sustenance; he was also responsible for the appearance of illness and death. Although the Bachwa believe that after people died, they were sent to the heavens to live with Djakomba, and they would not have to go through any adversity.

18. Dzivaguru

Among the Shona people of Zimbabwe, Dzivaguru is the god of water who also possessed ruling over the seasons and was apt to calling for the downpour of rain when he believed it to be necessary. The Shona people rely on the benevolence of the rain god, especially because a reliable source of rain is what ensures survival; therefore, they believed the rain deity to be quite generous and benevolent. They also believed that he was roaming around the land, using magic to perform various acts of kindness.

19. En-Kai

En-Kai means sky to the Massai people of Kenya. He is the supreme god and creator who brought forth rain and was also the deity of fecundity. He was a god of the sky and of the sun, while his wife Olapa was the goddess of the moon. The Massai people called him various names such as Parsai, meaning 'the one who is worshipped' and Emayian, which means 'the one who blesses.' The primeval man was created by the sky and sun deity and was called Naiteru-Kop; he and his wife were sent to the earth with livestock (sheep, cattle, and goats) to keep the earth and the natural resources within it for the sake of generations to come and thus, Naiteru-Kop and his family became the Massai ancestors.

A different tale holds that people came forth from a termite hole and decided to settle within the locality of the hole. A particular myth tells of the presentation of cattle to the Massai people; En-Kai told the primeval humans to leave their animal pens called *kraals* open at night, and while some obeyed, others did not. At night, noises from animals woke the people up, and when they looked outside, they saw cattle, goats, and sheep coming out of the termite hole and running into the *kraals* that were open. The Massai are the descendants of the people who left their *kraals* open, and those who did not are the present-day Kamba.

Another myth says that En-Kai asked Dorobo to go see him one morning. However, a Massai eavesdropped on the conversation and went to see En-Kai first. En-Kai believed the person to be Dorobo, and so he told the Massai to do a few things; after doing En-Kai's bidding, the Massai was to return to En-Kai in 3 days. Then, En-Kai eventually instructed the man to return to his hut and remain there no matter what; after that, En-Kai let down a rope made of pelt upon which cattle were sent to the earth. The Massai heard the noise and came out despite the warning. This broke the rope so that no more cattle were able to come down. Nevertheless, the Massai was contented with the ones he had gotten, explaining why the Massai had cattle while the Dorobo was forced to go hunting for wild game.

20. Eshu

Eshu or Esu is the god of chance, accident, and unpredictability of the Yoruba people of Nigeria. Amongst all the gods of the Yoruba people known as Orisa, he is one of the most important and complex. He had mastery of every language, and so he was the messenger of the supreme god, Olorun, who lived in the sky. Eshu was the mediator between humans and Olorun; he carried the messages and sacrifices of humans to Olorun. He also informed Olorun of the activities of both humans and the other gods, and whenever Olorun commanded it, Eshu delivered either penalties or rewards; furthermore, he gave an account of how worship and sacrifices were made. At the start of every rite, an offering had to be presented to Eshu, or else the ritual would fail. Eshu is believed to wait at gates and crossways, where he introduces chances and accidents into the lives of humans. Various myths tell of his intermediary role between forces that were in opposition, negotiating between the pantheon and re-establishing a balance in their relationship. The Yoruba's believe that divination – forecasting the future or fortune-telling – was handed down to them by Eshu. An aspect of Eshu portrays his benevolence and his protection, while another aspect of him shows him to be evil and his capability of leading humans to carry out evil activities.

One tale that exemplifies how much he enjoys stirring mischief shows how he caused a fight between two friends who both owned farms that bordered each other. Every single day, Eshu walked along the path, which separated both farms with a black cap on. Then a day came where he wanted to trick both men. He made a cap that had four colors (black, white, green, and red), which, contingent upon the angle it was seen, still appeared as one color. He put on his cap, with his pipe clung to his neck and staff to his back rather than his chest, he continued with his daily walk. The first farmer told his friend that he found it odd that Eshu was walking opposite the direction which he usually took when he walked in that path wearing a white cap rather than his usual black; his friend, on the other hand, answered saying that Eshu took his usual route while walking the path and that he was wearing a red cap. A fierce argument then broke out between the two, so they both went to visit their king to resolve the issue. While at the king's place, Eshu appeared and revealed that his cap had four colors and that if anyone was watching his pipe and staff instead of his feet, they would assume his motion was the opposite of what it actually was. Although he was naturally apt to causing dissension and strife, he always made a clean breast of his mischief in the end.

Eshu's mischief was not restricted to humans alone. He played tricks on the gods as well. A myth tells of how Obatala, who created land and humans, visited the god of thunder and lightning, Shango (Sango). Although Orunmila, who is the god of divination, had warned Obatala to not embark on the journey, Obatala insisted, and so Orunmila told him never to show any retaliation irrespective of what he faced. Obatala encountered Eshu on his way, who asked for Obatala's aid to place a bowl of palm oil upon his (Eshu's) head, while Obatala was helping to lift the bowl, oil spilled on his white garment. This forced him to go back home, change his garment and resume his journey; again, he encountered Eshu, who asked for his help to lift a bowl of oil, and when he did, the previous outcome was repeated. When the same thing happened the third time, Obatala did not change his garment but went on his journey; on his way, he saw one of Shango's horses which Eshu made to appear, running loose. Obatala caught the horse with the intention of returning it to Shango, but Shango's servants saw him first, and because of his dirty garments, they did not recognize him and taking him for a horse thief, they locked him in prison.

Many months and years went by while Obatala was in prison, and all through that time, he never protested. Soon, disaster fell upon the kingdom of Shango; rain never fell, and crops died. Upon consulting an oracle, Shango was told that someone was unjustly lying in his prison, and that was why the kingdom was suffering, and until that personality was released, the disasters would continue. Shango then visited his prison, and when he saw Obatala, he recognized him immediately and released him. Shango fell at the feet of Obatala and pleaded for pardon. Obatala granted his request, and rain once again fell in Shango's kingdom.

21. Gulu

Gulu is the sky god among the gods of the Baganda people of Uganda known as Lubaale, although the name was also used to refer to the heavens. Gulu was the next in hierarchy after the supreme deity, Katonda. Gulu fathered the god of death known as Walumbe, as well as Nambi that eventually married Kintu, the first king of Uganda.

22. Gurzil

Gurzil is the sun deity as well as the deity of prophecy to the Huwwara people of Libya. A two-horned Carthaginian (Carthage used to be an ancient city-state in the now Republic of Tunisia) god known as Baal Hammon is used to identify him and is represented with a bull. This deity was viewed as a guardian who, because of his precognition, served as a guide for humanity. The aspect that reflects him as a sun god was what made him able to drive out the darkness and bring light into the world.

23. Imana

Imana is the supreme god and creator of everything that exists as well as the omnipotent ruler of every living thing to the Banyarwanda, Hutu, and Tutsi people of Burundi and Rwanda. At the beginning of time, every living thing lived with him in the sky; death was not a lasting situation because Imana brought anyone who had died back to life within three days. One myth tells of a woman who had no child and begged the god for children; her wish was granted, and she bore three children with the condition that no one was to know where her children came from. Out of jealousy, the sister of the woman who had no children as well asked the woman to reveal how she got children and although she refused to tell for a while, she later revealed the secret to her sister. Imana's anger was kindled upon the woman because of her disobedience; the woman then killed her children so that she could quell his anger. The heavens opened and down fell the children to the earth, which was full of agony and asperity, and life was miserable for the children. After the woman and sister had asked the deity for pardon, he said he was going to bring them back to the sky when he felt they had gone through enough agony.

A story of how death came into existence suggests that death was personified as an animal that was hunted by Imana, who commanded humans to remain inside their houses while he hunted the animal so that death wouldn't have anywhere to hide. A certain woman visited her vegies garden, and death asked for her help, and she hid him underneath her skirt. Displeased by her disobedience, Imana declared that death would forever remain with humans.

Another tale says that death hid underneath the skirt of the woman, but she didn't know. Death went into the woman's house, and the woman passed away; the woman's death pleased her daughter-in-law. However, three days later, they saw that the grave of the woman was opened because Imana had brought the woman back to life, and she tried to resurrect. The daughter-in-law covered the soil to keep the woman in the grave; this happened day-after-day for three days, after which the grave grew silent. That the grave did not try to open again gave the daughter-in-law joy, but it also signified the permanence of death for humanity.

Another tale goes thus: A man was told that he would gain a long life from Imana if he was able to stay awake that night, but the man was unable to stay up. A snake eavesdropped on the conversation that Imana had with the man and went to wait on Imana; by mistaking the snake for the man, Imana said that when it grows old, it will be able to shed its skin and be born again. This is the reason why humans can die permanently while snakes are believed to have a long-lasting life.

24. Jok

Jok, also Jok Odudu, is the name given to the supreme deity and creator of the Acholi, Lango people of Uganda, the Alur people of the Democratic Republic of Congo and Uganda, and the Dinka people of Sudan. He was believed to possess ubiquity (he could be perceived in everything and every place). The celestial bodies are a part of his creation, so is the earth and everything that exists in it, including animals and humans to whom he taught agriculture and gave fire. He was also the god of fertility, and therefore, he made the ability to give birth possible. He sent down rain when humanity needed to grow their crops and ceased the rain so that humans could go hunting. His involvement in human matters was not direct as spirits who were also called *jok* were the ones who took part in the day-to-day activities of humans and accomplished the tasks that Jok wanted to be done. Lango culture believes that Jok was merged with the spirits, and so he was, in actuality, a combination of spirits in one deity.

A myth of how death came into existence tells that Jok intended to give humanity a fruit from the Tree of Life in order to make them immortal; when he invited them to the heavens to receive the fruit, they took time to respond, and this angered the supreme god, so he gave the fruit to the sun, the moon, and the stars. When the humans finally got to the heavens, Jok had no fruit left to give to them, and that is what explains why the celestial bodies are immortal, and the humans are not.

25. Juok

Juok, also Jwok is the supreme god and creator of the Anuak, Shilluk people of Sudan who are believed to have both male and female characteristics at the same time but usually referred to using 'he.' He birthed a lot of children such as an elephant, a buffalo, a lion, a crocodile, a dog and then the first humans, a boy and a girl. Juok became displeased with humanity, and he asked a dog to eliminate them; the dog, however, raised the children instead till they became adults. At the time, the earth became full of creatures, and the supreme god decided to group the creatures, assign them to a particular area of land together to provide them with weapons. Humans were the last he considered, and seeing this, the dog cognized that by the time Juok would be done, there would be no land or weapons left for humans, so he told the man to go tell the supreme god that he (man) was the elephant, lion, and buffalo; hearing this, Juok gave the man all the spears. At the arrival of the animals, there were no weapons left, so Juok gave the tusks to the elephant, claws to the lion, teeth to the crocodile, and horns to the buffalo. Using his spears, the man chased the animals and took for himself the best land.

A tale of how death came to be said that at the beginning of time, death was not a lasting situation. People usually died and returned back to life after three days. Juok, one day, decided that death should be the final end for one's life, and so he threw a rock into the river. The dog asked humanity to get the rock out, but no one paid him any attention. The dog couldn't get the rock out himself; however, he was able to break a huge part of it and took it home. Since then, humans started dying permanently, although because a huge part of the rock was broken, they could live long before they died.

26. Kalumba

Kalumba is to the Luba people of the Democratic Republic of the Congo, the supreme god, and creator who, at the beginning of time, sent a man and woman on an exploration of the universe. The man and woman found the place to be dark save for the presence of the moon, and they returned to him with the information, after which Kalumba made the sun to serve as a light for humans. He again sent the man and woman back to the earth with a dog, birds, spark rocks, iron, and the ability to reproduction, thus making them humanity's earliest parents.

Another tale says that humans lived with Kalumba in the beginning, but they had started fighting, so the god sent them to the earth where they first felt hunger, cold, illness, and death. Having being told by a diviner to return to the heavens to escape their predicament, humans built a high tower that reached the sky; on getting there, they beat drums to let the rest of humanity on earth know that they had gotten to their destination. Angered by the noise, the deity reduced the tower to rubble so no more humans could get to where he was.

A myth of the existence of death says that Kalumba was aware that both life and death would be on the same path to get to humanity, so he sent a goat and a dog to act as sentries on the path and let only life through in a bid to make humans immortals. An argument broke out between the dog and the goat regarding who would stand guard first. The goat pointed out that the dog would sleep off before yielding and allowing the dog to stand guard. It happened as the goat anticipated.

Death slipped past because the dog slept off. When it was the goat's time to keep watch, it did not sleep, so it saw life when it tried to pass, although he did not know death had already gotten into the world.

27. Kanu

Kanu is the name given to the supreme god and creator of the Limba people of Sierra Leone. The different groups of the Limba have different names for the deity; the Safroko Limba called him Kanu, the Sela Limba called him Masala, and the Tonko Limba call him Masaranka. At the beginning of time, Kanu was living on earth, and then, creatures began attacking each other, and this displeased him, and even though the deity commanded that this be stopped, a python killed a deer and ate it. Then, ants ate the python, the fire destroyed the ants, and water quenched the fire; all of these occurrences made Kanu exile himself to the sky.

The story of how death came into being goes thus: Kanu had created a medicinal drug to make humans immortal, which he gave to a serpent to deliver it to humans, but a toad took the drug, and while it was hopping, all of the drug splattered. Kanu declined creating another drug, and then death came to Limba.

28. Katonda

Katonda is the name of the supreme deity of the Baganda people of Uganda. He was recognized as the father of the Baganda pantheon in the same manner as the first king, Kintu is recognized as the father of all living humans on earth. The Baganda thought of Katonda as a benevolent deity who preserved life and never brought harm or death to humans. He was the ultimate judge of humans, and the natural world was presided over by him via the spirits of deified heroes, incarnations of natural elements, and ancestors.

29. Khonvoum

Khonvoum is to the pygmy of Cameroon, Central African Republic, the Democratic Republic of the Congo, Gabon, and the Republic of the Congo; the supreme god and creator – most significant god among all the pygmy gods. He is also recognized as the god of the hunt and 'the great hunter'; his bow was made from two snakes, and it looked like the rainbow to humans. Humans were only able to contact this deity through an elephant named Gor – another myth says it's a chameleon. After he had created the universe, Kibuka let down to the earth, the primeval humans; legend has it that he created black people from black clay, white people from white clay, and used red clay to create pygmies. Pygmies live as hunters and gatherers in the bleak forests in Africa, and ten different populations exist, such as Aka, Ake, Baka, Benzele, Bongo, Efe, Gvelli, Mbuti, Tikar, and Tswa. Khovoum made provisions of animals and exuberant forest vegetation for them all; at night, the task of the god was to renew the sun so it could rise the following day. To do this, fragments of stars were collected by Khovoum, and he chucked them to the sun to revitalize it.

30. Kibuka

Kibuka is the god of war amongst all the gods of the Baganda people of Uganda. Humans conferred with the deity when they had to face an enemy and defend themselves. One myth of this people says that it was the deity's refusal to pay close attention to admonitions that resulted in his death. His brother, Mukasa sent him to the earth to aid Baganda people when they had to war against Nyoro, warning him not to let his enemies know his location and to never contact the women of Nyoro. On the first day of battle, Kibuka hid in a cloud and was firing arrows at the Nyoro people; the first day's battle was won by the Baganda, and they took Nyoro people, including women, as spoils. Kibuka had one woman sent to him, but she fled at night after discovering all his secrets and told the Nyoro people; the following day during the battle, archers of Nyoro launched a fusillade of arrows toward the cloud where Kibuka was hiding, which wounded him mortally.

31. Kiumbi

Kiumbi is the supreme god and creator of the Asu people in the Pare region of Tanzania. The supreme god is said to live in the sky like many of the gods in Africa. Kiumbi used to be close to the humans that he made, but because of their disobedience, he separated himself a great deal away from them, and the only means by which humans could commune with him was through the ancestors who acted as mediators between him (Kiumbi) and them (humans). The humans then sought to restore the proximity that existed between them and the deity, and to achieve this, they attempted to build a tower that reached the sky, but as they got closer to him, he went farther away. The more they tried to get close to him, it upset him so he sent a famine upon the earth, which killed every person on the earth save a boy and a girl from whom the new human race stemmed.

32. Kwoth

Kwoth is the supreme god and creator of the Nuer people of Sudan. Kwoth didn't particularly have any form to him, nor did he have a particular place where he stayed. Being Kwoth Nhial, which means a 'spirit who is in the sky', he was usually affiliated with and believed to reveal himself via all the bodies in the sky, which include the sun, the moon, and stars, as well as natural occurrences. The people believed that he fell in the rain, blew in the wind, and that he was also within thunder and lightning. The rainbow was referred to as 'god's necklace.'

Like many other myths of African civilizations, the Nuer people also believe that heaven and earth used to be connected with a rope, and at the time, there was no death. Whenever a person became old, they could use the rope to climb up to heaven for the deity to make them young again and then have them return to earth. On a certain day, however, a hyena climbed up the rope to the sky, and the Kwoth asked the spirits in the sky to keep a close watch on the hyena and stop it from returning to the earth because that could cause problems. But, the hyena somehow broke away, and on its way down, it severed the rope, hence cutting the link with the sky and the earth, and people could not climb up to the heavens anymore and be returned to their young selves and death entered the world.

33. Legba

Among the gods of the Fon people, Legba is the seventh and last son of the Mawu-Lisa, the creator. When Mawu-Lisa had divided up the regions of the world among her first six children, there was nothing left to give to Legba, so the creator made him her messenger. His job was to visit the domains of the other gods and then return with information to Mawu-Lisa, and for that purpose, Legba had the gift of being able to speak various languages so that if anybody, whether human or deity who wanted to convey a message to the supreme god, they could easily give the message to him and he would deliver it. Furthermore, he was in possession of the key to the gate that separated the world of humanity from the domain of the deities, and when it came to deciding the destiny of humans, he had a major role to play.

Legba was known to be very intelligent and crafty. There was a time when Mawu-Lisa sent him to earth to check on the god of the earth, Sagbata, who informed Legba that Hevioso (Sogbo) was preventing rain. Legba assured the earth god that he would inform Mawu-Lisa and then send a bird called Wutulu with instructions on how to proceed. Wutulu then came to Sagbata, telling him to build a great fire with smoke that would reach the heavens, and when Sagbata started the fire, Legba went to Mawu-Lisa with the message that the earth was on fire, so Mawu-Lisa ordered Hevioso to release rain on the earth. Legba was originally the reason why it stopped raining on the earth when he told Mawu-Lisa that there wasn't enough water in the heavens, and that was what led to the ceasing of a downpour.

34. Pishiboro

This is the supreme god of the Igwike people of Botswana, Namibia. At the beginning of time, the only thing in existence was just emptiness save for the supreme god Pishiboro. It was his death that brought about the creation of the universe. Legend has it that a puff adder bit the supreme god, and that was what killed him; the rocks and hills were created from the blood that poured out of his injures, and valleys were carved from his flailing body. Rivers and streams were created from the water that poured out of his body, and his hair formed the clouds from which the rain which gave life poured down.

After his resurrection, Pishiboro then created humans, and being unhappy with how they looked without hair, he gave them hair; but that only made them look like other animal creatures, so he made them again with hair only on certain parts of their bodies. After that, the supreme god shaped all the animals he had created into various forms, gave them names and functions. He then declared that all animals having horns were to be consumed as food; humans were not to be consumed. If they died of natural causes or were killed, they should be buried.

Goddesses

1. Abuk

Abuk is a goddess of the Dinka people of Sudan. This is the primeval woman whose status was raised up to the divine level so that she became the patron goddess of women and gardens. Abuk was in charge of handling any and all issues that concerned women, which included, for the most part, the growing of millet. A small snake is an allegory that is used to represent her. It is said that at the beginning of time, there was a rope linking the heavens, which were home to the supreme god, Nhialic, to the earth. The supreme god gave his permission for Abuk and her husband Garang (primeval man) to plant and grind a single millet a day to be consumed as food; however, a certain day came where Abuk became so hungry, in fact, that she planted a lot of millet cereals. She was made use of a hoe for her cultivation, and in the process, she struck Nhialic with her hoe by accident because the earth and the heavens were in close proximity; furious about this, Nhialic then severed the rope that linked the heavens to the earth and decided to longer meddle in human affairs.

As a result of this outcome, humans are forced to toil intensely in order for them to have food; furthermore, things like sicknesses and death found its way into the world. Some traditions believe that Abuk was the mother of a rain and fertility god by the name of Deng, who also is the one who mediates between humans and the supreme god.

2. Ala

Ala is also called Ale or Ali among the Igbo people in Nigeria. It is the name given to the earth goddess, who is also the goddess of fertility and daughter of the supreme god – Chukwu. Despite the fact that humans were created by Chukwu, he was distant from them; this is what differentiates between him and Ala because, unlike Chukwu, she was close to humans that she came to be recognized as the mother of the Igbo people. It is said that everything was brought forth from her – the earth was borne from her womb – and she took over the protection of the inhabitants of the earth. Since being the goddess of fertility, she made the female of the human species able to give birth, give life to children, and kept watch over them through their lifetime. She accepted people who died into her body (earth) and ruled over the ancestors because the rulership of the underworld belonged to her. The Igbo people believe that when a person dies, they become the earth and become one with Ala.

3. Ama

Ama or Ma is the name given to the creator – who may be a combination of two gods – among the Jukun people of Nigeria. At times, Ama has two aspects: a god (male) and a goddess (female). The female aspect of Ama is the Earth goddess believed to be the mother of the universe and counterpart of Chido, the sky god. Chido was the god that resided in the sky while Ama resided on the earth. Ama was the creator of the heavens, the earth, and everything that exists; since being the earth personified, she ruled the underworld known as Kindo, of which the Jukun people believe that every living thing originated from and where they will return to when they die. Ama is equated as a potter; it is said that she created the body of humans by building it up bone after bone, just as a potter makes a pot by building up clay. When Ama was done creating any human, Chido would descend from the sky and breathed life into the person so that they could come alive. When Ama created crops to give humans nourishment, Chido sent rain to help grow the crops.

4. Asaase Yaa

Asaase Yaa, also known as Aberewa or Asase Ya, is a goddess of the barren places of the earth among the Ashanti people of Ghana. She is the daughter of Nyame, the supreme god and creator, and some versions of her story say she is the mother of Asansi, the spider, a trickster, and a culture hero. Asaase Yaa or Aberewa had a long, sharp sword that was self-controlled to fight as long as she gave the order, and whenever she did, the sword killed everyone it ran into unless she ordered the sword to stop.

A tale of Anansi and Aberewa's sword goes thus: famine existed in the land, and the only storehouse that had food belonged to Nyame, so Anansi offered to become Nyame's agent and sell the food in his storehouse in exchange for Anansi's head to be shaved on a daily basis. Anansi always felt pain when his head was shaved, and people mocked his looks; so, he stole some of Nyame's food and ran to Asaase Yaa's house. He then asked her to protect him, and she agreed. A day came when the goddess left the house, and Anansi stole her sword and went back to Nyame, offering to protect him using the sword, should Nyame ever need protecting and Nyame gave his consent. When faced with enemies, Anansi commanded the sword to fight, and the army of the enemy was vanquished, but then Anansi forgot the words he had to utter to make the sword stop, and since the sword could not be stopped, it also destroyed Nyame's forces and killed Anansi as well. The sword then bound itself to the ground and turned into a plant that had sharp leaves, which can cut anyone that touches them. Since no one ever ordered the sword to stop, the plant still cuts people to date.

Chapter 5
Legends with animals as protagonists

Anansi

The tales of Anansi is one that is found throughout West Africa, with the ones originating from Ghana being among the best of tales. Anansi was an Akan folktale character, which means spider because it often assumed the shape of a spider. Anansi was considered to be a god of all knowledge of stories. He was a trickster who was well known for his creative and cunning nature. His ability to triumph and outsmart over more powerful opponents often portrayed him as a protagonist.

From Ghana, Anansi spread to Suriname, West Indies, Sierra Leone, where they were introduced by Jamaican Maroons, the Netherlands Antilles, Aruba, and Curacao.

Over time, Anansi had been represented with different names in many different ways like "Kwaku Ananse", "Ananse", "Anancy". Now, it is depicted as "Ba Anansi", "Kompa Nanzi", "Nancy, Aunt Nancy or Sis Nancy". Though often depicted as an animal, Anansi's representation also includes acting and appearing as a man. This gives a clue that Anansi was an anthropomorphized spider with the face of a man or a man with spider-like features.

In other folktales, Anansi had a family which included his long-suffering wife, Okonore Yaa. Other regions knew her as Aso, Shi Maria, or Crooky. His firstborn son's name was Ntikuma. Tikelenkelen was his big-headed son. Afudohwedohwe was his pot-bellied son, while his son with spindly neck and legs was known as Nankonhwea. Also, not leaving out his beautiful daughter Anansewa whom Anansi in Efua's tale embarked on a mission to ensure she got the right suitor.

Anansi is synonymous with skill and wisdom in speech because his stories were exclusively part of an oral tradition. Anansi stories came to the limelight and was a major part of the Ashanti oral culture, which was seen in their kinds of fables, as was proven by R.S. Rattray's work recorded in both Twi language and English. Even Peggy Appiah attested that: "So well-known is he that he has given name to the rich tradition of tales on which so many Ghanaian children are brought up anansesem or spider tales."

The rest of the world came about the tales of Anansi through oral tradition. Most especially are the Caribbean people who were made aware of these tales by those who were enslaved during the Atlantic slave trade. Rather than the importance of Anansi to diminish socially, it became celebrated as a symbol of slave survival and resistance. The reasons being that Anansi was able to use his cunningness and trickery to turn the tables of oppression. This was a system used by slaves at that time to gain the upper hand from their taskmasters in the plantation environment.

The inspiring strategy of resistance, Anansi's tales were able to play multifunctional roles in the lives of slaves, thereby enabling enslaved Africans to establish a sense of continuity with their African past and offering them hope to transform and assert their identity within the boundaries of captivity. As was argued in historian Lawrence W. Levine's Black Culture and Consciousness, Africans enslaved in the new world majorly devoted "the structure and message of their tales to the compulsions and needs of their present situation."

Since Jamaica had the largest concentration of enslaved Ashanti, the version of Anansi's stories well preserved are those of the Jamaicans, and relating to their Ashanti origins, each story carries their own proverbs at the end. There is a proverb at the end of the story "Anansi and Brah Dead" that suggests that Anansi in times of slavery was referred to by his original Akan name: "Kwaku Anansi" or

"Kwaku" being used interchangeably with Anansi. The proverb is: "If yuh cyan ketch Kwaku, yuh ketch him shut". This points to the time when the personification of death Brah Dead (the brother death or dry-bones) was chasing Anansi to kill him.

The proverb meaning: The target of revenge and destruction, even killing, will be anyone close to the intended, such as family members and loved ones.

In the diaspora, based on his penchant for ingenuity, Anansi's presence has been reinvented through an exchange that is multi-ethnic and beyond its Akan-Ashanti origin, seen in the diversity of names attributed to Anansi in his stories. From "Kuenta Di Nazi" to "Anansi-tori". Or is the 'Ti Bouki" character, the buffoon who was harassed constantly by "Ti Malice" or is it the Haitian trickster "Uncle Mischief" associated with Anansi references ti's exchange: "Bouki" is a word descending from the Wolof language referencing the hyena indigenous to them. Anansi roles beyond the era of slavery entertain just as they instruct, showing alongside his flaws, cleverness, and features the subversive just as the mundane. Anansi has now become both an idea that inspires and a cautionary tale against selfish desires that can lead to one's undoing. He is now evolved and considered a classical hero as compared to being seen as a trickster.

Popular Anansi stories

There exist many stories collected in the literature that have Anansi written all over it. Among which are;

Akan-Ashanti stories

How the sky-God stories became Anansi

This is Rattray version of the most commonly retold folktales as recorded in his book The Akan-Ashanti fork tales. In these tales, there were no stories in the world because the sky God Nyame, also known as Nyankonpon, had all the stories. Anansi wanted Nyame's stories, so he then went ahead to see the sky god so as to offer him money for his stories. Nyame was not convinced at Anansi proposition because other great kingdoms like Bekwai, Kokofu, and Asumengya had tried to do the same as well but could not pull it off. So, he was wondering how

Anansi would succeed when others had failed. Anansi was not intimidated, rather he promised to do whatever it cost, and so, he went ahead to ask the sky god to name his price. Nyame played along since Anansi was so insistent.

Nyame's high price was the impossible labor he set, knowing that Anansi wouldn't be able to get the task done. The task was that Anansi had to capture four of the most dangerous creatures in the world, namely Osebo the Leotard, the fairy Mmoatia, the Mmaboron Hornets, and Onini, the python. Anansi promised to get the four dangerous creatures and even throw in his mother Ya Nsia as a bonus. Nyame encouraged him to be on his way, having accepted Anansi offer while Anansi, on the other hand, went about putting his schemes to motion.

First, Anansi went to his family and then told them about his plans, not excluding his mother also. He then sought the counsel of his wife Aso as to how to go about capturing Onini, the python. Aso told him to cut a branch from a palm tree along with strings creeper vine. Then he should head to the river where Onini stays, pretending to have been in a heated argument with her as touching the size and height of Onini's body that it was longer than the branch of a palm-tree. All this attempt was set at getting Onini's attention, thereby enabling his capture.

So, Anansi set out just as his wife had counseled him. On his way to Onini's place, he began to argue imaginatively that his wife claimed that Onini's body was longer than a full-grown palm tree branch. Onini overheard Anansi's argument and came out to find out what was going on. Having explained all to Onini, he decided to assist Anansi in proving that he was longer than the branch of a palm tree. This, he agreed to do unaware of Anansi's scheme. When he inquired what he should do, Anansi told him to go stretch against the branch of the palm-tree he had already cut down.

On stretching against the branch of the palm-tree, Anansi took the string creeper vine to tie Onini completely. Having done that, Anansi wasted no time in going over to Nyame's. It was on his way to Nyame's that he told Onini of the deal he has made. Nyame was quite impressed with Anansi's victory but also reminded him of the remaining three challenges, secretly rooting that Anansi would meet with failure soon.

Anansi went home to his wife to let her know of the successful capture of Onini. Now, he needed her counsel once again to capture Mmoboro Hornets, of which she gladly obliged him. She told Anansi to fill a gourd with water and take it to the Hornets, which Anansi did. Heading into the bush, he came across a swarm of hornets. Having crept to where the hornets were, he sprinkled some of the water on the gourd at the Mmoboro Hornets while he immersed himself in the remaining water.

Anansi then cut a banana leaf to cover his head. Out of anger, the Hornets flew to where Anansi was hiding. Anansi, removing the banana leaf from his head, told the Hornets that it had been raining, showing them the wet banana leaf as proof. He then told the Hornets that the only way they can avoid the danger called rain was for them to get into the gourd. This idea sounded nice to the Hornets.

Unaware of Anansi's intention, they all flew into the gourd. Quickly, Anansi covered the mouth of the gourd and set out to see the Sky God. Anansi then told the Hornets of his plan to trade them for the Sky God's stories, for at this time, it was already too late for the Hornets. The Sky God accepted the Hornets from Anansi, congratulated him for his success thus far then reminded him that the task is far from completion. Anansi, leaving the Sky God's place, headed home.

On getting home, Anansi told his companion of his success. Now Osebo the Leopard was his next target. As usual, his wife counseled him. This time around, she told him to dig a hole and then cover it to catch the Leopard. Having understood the plan, he left home to where Osebo the Leopard was always found. Anansi dug a big hole around the place and then covered it with brushwood, knowing that there was no way the Leopard would miss stumbling into the hole. Coming back the next morning, just as he has predicted, he found the Leopard in the pit. Feigning ignorance and sympathetic at the same time asked the Leopard if he was drunk since he had once cautioned the Leopard about his drinking. Anansi then offered to help the Leopard but claimed that he was afraid for his life, saying that if he helped the Leopard out of the pit, the Leopard was going to eat him. The Leopard promised not to harm him, and so Anansi reached for his knife, cut down two long sticks, and began to let it down into the hole. As the Leopard was attempting to scale the sticks and escape, Anansi threw his knife at the Leopard, and the haft of his knife hit the Leopard on the head, rendering him unconscious.

Anansi then went in to capture the Leopard. Just like the other victims of Anansi's schemes, he never failed to tell them his deal with the Sky God and how he desired to get the Sky God's stories. Nyame, receiving the Leopard from Anansi, still was not convinced that Anansi could accomplish all his tasks.

Anansi returning home, decided another time to capture Mmoatia the Fairy. Thinking through on how to capture the Fairy, Anansi came up with the idea of carving an Akua doll. Then Anansi got some sap from a gum tree and rubbed it on the doll till it became very sticky. Anansi was not so satisfied with what he had done, so he pounded some mashed yams (eto) and cover the doll's hand with it.

He then filled a basin with some mashed yams and tied some of his silk around the doll's waist so as to manipulate it. Having been satisfied with his creation, he headed straight to the land of fairies and placed the Akua doll in front of the Odum tree, majorly where fairies congregated with the basin and eto in front as bait.

This he did while he waited for the fairies behind the Odum tree. Soon, some fairies came along, with one lured away from her sister. On getting to where the Akua doll was, the fairy implored the doll if she could have some of her eto, Anansi then tugs the string around the doll's waist, causing it to nod her head in response. The fairy then quickly went to her sister and asked for permission to eat some eto, which they agreed.

The Mmoatia went back to the Akua doll and ate to her fill, and after which, she thanked the Akua doll, but this time did not get a response because Anansi refused to tug the string. The Mmoatia was not pleased by the attitude of Akua doll, so she called out to her sisters, who advised her to slap the doll. On doing that, her hand got stuck.

The Mmoatia beckoned on her sisters, who then encouraged her to use her other hand, and again, the second hand got stuck on the face of the Akua doll. Once more, the Mmoatia called out to her sisters, and this time they advised her to bludgeon the doll with the rest of her body and that she would be successful. This, she also did and was completely married to the Akua doll. Anansi came out from his hiding place and used the remaining string to tie the fairy to the doll.

Quickly, Anansi went back home to his mother and reminded her of his agreement with the Sky God for his stories, and she was part of the deal. His mother complied and went alongside him and Mmoatia to go see Nyame. Anansi presented both his mother and the Mmoatia to Nyame, who was now really amazed at the spider's success. Nyame then summoned the elders of his kingdom, the Akwam chiefs, the Kontire, the Adontem general of his army, the Oyoko, Ankobea, Kyidom, and lastly, the Gyase.

The Sky God then told everyone present of the task he gave to Anansi and presented the evidence, including Anansi's mother Ya Nsia before everyone and how Anansi was able to accomplish all when other great kingdoms had failed. He then relinquished the rights to his stories, that they would no longer be called by his name anymore.

From then onward, the Sky-God's stories became Anansi's stories and would be known as the spider stories for eternity. The people rejoiced alongside Nyame that day at Anansi's victory, and that is why every story, no matter the theme, is called a Spider story.

Take note that they exist substantial variants of this tale, like Haley's omitting Aso and Ya Nsia while retelling it. The Tiger became the one from whom the stories came from, according to a Caribbean version. Another common version presented Mmoatia as a solitary fairy that can turn invisible. Another version that exists does not require Anansi to capture a python.

Lightning Bird

The Impundulu, which is translated as "lightning bird" or Thekwane (or Izulu) is a folklore creature of the tribes of South Africa, which includes the Zulu, the Xhosa, and the Pondo. The Impundulu assumed the form of a black and white bird, having the size of a person capable of summoning lightning and thunder with its wings and talons. The bird is a vampiric in nature affiliated with witchcraft. The impundulu, being the servant of a witch doctor, attacks the witch's enemies. Its taste for blood is insatiable and does take the form of a handsome man to seduce women.

The hammer-kop, among certain African tribes, is believed to be the true lightning bird. While others believed that the true lightning bird only manifests itself through lightning, only in rare cases does it show up as a bird, and that is when it wants to reveal itself to women. With this many forms, the bird's true nature is imaginary; Like the village girl that described the bird that ran up to her hole and left claw marks on her body before flying into the clouds to be a black rooster-like bird. At another place, the lightning bird was described as having feathers like those of a peacock or a fiery red tail, bill, and legs.

The lightning bird has been described as a winged creature with the size of a man by most persons who have sighted the bird in one or another. Other than it being a huge black and white bird of prey, it is also said that the bird does mask itself as a man when need be.

Power

The fats of the bird can either be considered as a valuable component for traditional medicine or as the fuel needed by the bird when it wants to set things on fire by throwing down a lightning strike. One can come about this fat in two ways, either by catching the bird at the point when the lightning strikes the ground or by digging the bird up from an underground cavity at the spot. Furthermore, the bird is believed to lay large eggs underground at the very spot of the lightning strike. Now this laying of eggs could serve as a good or bad omen when the ground is dug to procure the eggs or dispose of it. The bird is also compared to a vampire because it is immortal. Legend has it that not only does the bird outlives its masters, but it can also equally be passed from mother to daughter carrying out the bidding of its owner. This bird cannot be killed by stabbing or gunshots. It cannot be poisoned or even drowned. The only known weakness of the lightning bird is that it can be killed by fire.

Cultural Significant

The witch doctor, as it is seen in most tribes, is the only one that has the essential role of dealing with the lightning bird. Also, a supposed extract from the flesh of the bird can be used by the witch doctor to track thieves, mind control both law-abiding citizens and criminal masterminds in that society. The lightning bird is the witch confidant as it is most times seen on the back of witches that turned themselves into a hyena. The impundulu is considered the witch right-hand man as it is greatly feared. It can wreck-havoc, cause illness, and bring bad luck to a person when it is dispatched by a witch to do her bidding.

Other Vampire birds

The lightning bird has similarities with the vampire finch, which is confined to the Galapagos Islands. According to legend, the lightning bird is a vampire bird that feeds on blood. For instance, it feeds off other birds in animal form and, while in a human form, feeds off humans. The vampire finch, on the other hand, draws blood from sleeping sea birds by pecking them at the base of their feathers. There is another bird found in Africa called the red-billed Oxpecker.

This bird can be seen on cattle whenever there is fresh blood. Among these birds that have a taste for blood, none is as dangerous as the lightning bird.

A South African man in 2005 was convicted of culpable homicide after killing a two- year old whom he believed to be a lightning bird but in human form.

Chapter 6
Legends with heroes as protagonists

These are kings, queens, chiefs, and other leaders all across the continent of Africa who stood and fought, laying down their lives for what they believed. Among these heroes are:

King Sekhukhune 1881

In the year 1861, after the death of his father Sekwati I, Sekhukhune became the king of the Pedi or Bapedi nation, usurping Mampuru II, the supposed heir to the throne of the Pedi nation.

In 1881, he was arrested in the ZAR capital in Pretoria after he waged war against the Boer of the South African Republic, the British empire, and the Swazi. He met with defeat at the hand of the British and 10,000 Swazi warriors.

On August 29th, 1882, the London Times, usually not known for writing on African ruling Affairs, wrote a tribute to Sekhukhune after he was assassinated by Mampuru II in 1882. Mampuru, on the other hand, was later hanged in Pretoria by ZAR the year following.

Shango of the Oyo Empire

Shango was the king who brought prosperity to the Yoruba people of the Oyo empire. He was the third king of the Oyo empire and has so many stories and myths surrounding him. For many Afro-Caribbean religions, Shango stands as the cornerstone of them all.

According to the Yoruba religion, Shango (Changó or Xangô in Latin America), is one of the principal ancestors of the Yoruba people and the popular Orisha of thunder. He is considered a focal point in the Santeria religion of the Caribbean as he represents the Oyo people of West Africa. During the Atlantic slave trade, the Oyo empire sold people, a lot of whom were then taken to South America and the Caribbean. This is the main reason why any Orisha initiation ceremony performed anywhere across the New World within the past hundred years has always been done according to the ancient traditional ceremony performed in the Oyo empire. This is the most complete traditional ceremony that has arrived on the shores of America.

Shango's sacred number is 6, while the color "red and white" are his sacred colors. Oshe is his symbol, which is a representation of swift and balanced justice. In general, Shango is the owner of the art of dance, the beta (3 double-headed drums), and music.

Jaja of Opobo

Early Life

Jubo Jubogha as he was named by his first master, was born in Igbo land and was sold as a slave to Bonny trader at the age of twelve. Later on, he was sold to the powerful head of the Opobu Manila Group of Chief Alali. This enterprising and gifted individual called Jaja by the British eventually became one of the most powerful men in the eastern Niger Delta.

The Niger Delta was the site of unique settlements called city-states. It is where Niger empties itself into the Gulf of Guinea in a system of intricate waterways.

Like the other city-states, Bonny rose to prominence and gained its wealth from the profits of the slave trade right from the 15th to the 18th centuries. In Bonny, anyone who was successful in business could attain prestige and power. As for Jaja's case, a hard-working slave could work his way up to the head of state because the house was a socio-political entity and was the basic unit of the city-state.

After the abolition of the slave trade in 1807, the trade-in oil which dethroned the trade-in slave began to reign in the 19th century. This trade became so lively that the region was called the Oil River areas.

Since the producers in the hinterland were prohibited from trading directly with the Europeans on the coast, the Houses of Bonny and other city-states controlled the palm oil trade both internally and externally. The Europeans were afraid of malaria and, as such, their reason for never leaving the coast.

The Rise of King Jaja

Jaja quickly became the head of the Anna Pepple House, absorbing other houses and increasing its activities as well as its influence because he was shrewd in business and politics. Soon, he increased operations in the hinterland and a growing number of European contacts. Because of a power tussle among rival factions in the houses at Bonny, the faction led by Jaja went its own way, thereby establishing a new settlement called Opobo. He declared his independence from Bonny and became King Jaja Opobo.

Opobo was strategically located between the production areas of the hinterland and Bonny, which King Jaja capitalized on in controlling trade and politics in the Niger Delta. This he did that at the end of his ascendancy, fourteen out of eighteen Bonny houses had relocated to Opobo.

Jaja became so wealthy and powerful in a few years that he was now shipping palm oil by himself directly to Liverpool. British consul was not pleased with this latest development, so Jaja was offered a treaty of protection that, in return, the chiefs surrendered their sovereignty. Jaja refused and was assured rather vaguely that nothing would happen to his authority nor sovereignty of Opobo.

The Scramble for Africa and the fall of Jaja

Jaja continued on the path of regulating trades and levy duties on British traders. He went as far as stopping trade on the river till one British firm paid the levy duties. Despite British threats to destroy Opobo through bombing, Jaja refused to yield to the order of the British Consul to put an end to these activities. The scramble for Africa had already taken place unknown to Jaja and Opobo was now part of British territories. In this era, gunboat diplomacy was the method of settling international issues, and Great Britain fancied using her Naval power to negotiate terms that were more favorable to her people.

Jaja was arrested and sent to Accra when he was lured aboard the British Consul's warship. He was back to St. Vincent (Saint Vincent and the Grenadines), West Indies, after he was tried and found guilty of blocking the highways of trade and breaking the trade treaty. He died en route, four years later when he was permitted to return to Nigeria from exile.

Jaja exposed the British imperialism through his effective resistance and persevering insistence on African independence. He became the first victim who had suffered in the hands of foreign territorial intrusion. The news of Jaja and what became of him in the hands of Britain quickly spread like wildfire throughout the whole Niger Delta that other Chiefs, out of fear, surrendered quickly.

The British trader wasted no time in boycotting the middleman and dealing directly with the palm oil producers as soon as Quinine was discovered as the cure of malaria. This led to the decline of the city-states.

The death of Jaja was a victory for Britain as it eventually led to the colonization of the Niger Delta region before the end of that century.

Queen Amina of Zaria

The heart of the Hausa realm comprises of the seven original Hausa lands. This includes Daura, Katsina, Kano, Zazzau, Gobir, Garun Gabas, and Rano, which covers an area of approximately 1,300 square kilometers. In the 16th century, the capital of Zazzau was built by the Queen Bakwa Turunku and named it after her youngest daughter. The state of Zazzau was later renamed Zaria, which in present-day Nigeria is a province and a traditional kingdom.

However, the Legendary Amina, the elder daughter of Queen Bakwa, was the one that inherited her mother's warlike nature. At age 16, Amina (or Aminatu) was given the traditional title of Magajiya when her mother was made a queen. Magajiya was a title that speaks of honor and respect meant for the daughters of the Monarch. Amina was known for her bravery and military exploits as she spent time developing her military skills. A song was even written in her honor to celebrate "Amina, the daughter of Nikatau as a woman capable of doing what a man can do."

The architectural design that created the strong earthen walls surrounding her city was credited to Amina. This is a prototype used for the fortification in all Hausa states. Later, many of these fortified walls, known as Ganuwar Amina or Amina's walls, were built around the territories she had conquered.

Every of her conquest was of two folds; the first was to extend her nation beyond its main borders, and the second one was to reduce each conquered city to a position of a vassal.

It was stated by Sultan Muhammad Bello of Sokoto that "She made war upon these countries and overcame them totally so that the people of Katsina paid tribute to her and the men of Kano". She also made war on cities of Bauchi till her kingdom reached the sea in the south and the west." Likewise, according to the chronicle of Kano, she led her armies as far as Nupe." "The Sarkin Nupe sent her (i.e., the princess) 40 eunuchs as well as 10,000 kola nuts. She was the first in the Hausa land to own eunuchs and kola nuts."

In as much as Amina was a notable gimbiya (Princess), there exist so many theories as to the time of her reign. Some theories even doubt if she was ever Queen, to begin with. While one theory is of the view that she reigned from approximately 1536 to 1573. Another says that she became a queen right after her brother, Karama's death in 1576. While yet another one claims that she was never a titular queen even though she was a de facto ruler and a princess.

One thing is certain, despite the inconsistencies in these theories and that's over a 34 years period, the border of Zaira was extended greatly through her many conquests and the incorporation of territories conquered. As a result of the extension of Zaira beyond its primary borders and its growth in prominence, it became the center of the North-South Sahara trade and East-West Sudan trade.

Queen Nzingha of Ndongo (1582–1663)

Nzinga of Ndongo and Matamba

The Portuguese stake in the slave trade was threatened in the 16th century by both France and England, and for that reason, the Portuguese relocated their trading activities southward towards Congo and South-West Africa. In the final phase of their conquest of Angola, the Portuguese met with stiff opposition from a head of state, a queen who was equally a military leader.

Professor Glasgow, of Bowie Maryland, outlined some important aspects of her life: "Her extraordinary story begins about 1582, the year of her birth. She was referred to as Nzingha, or Jinga, but was better known as Ann Nzingha. She was the sister of the then-reigning King of Ndongo, Ngoli Bbondi, whose country was later called Angola. Nzingha was from an ethnic group called the Jagas. The Jagas was an extremely militant group who formed a human shield against the Portuguese slave traders. Nzingha never accepted the Portuguese conquest of Angola and was always on the military offensive. As part of her strategy against the invaders, she formed an alliance with the Dutch, who she intended to use to defeat the Portuguese slave traders.

Nzinga became Queen of Ndongo in 1623 at the age of 41. She preferred to be called a king and, as such, forbade her people from calling her Queen. She loved dressing in a man's clothing when leading her armies to war.

Later on, in her life, in the year 1659, at the age of seventy-five, she signed a treaty with the Portuguese, which in any way brought her no Joy. Nzinga resisted and fought the Portuguese all through her adult life until her death in 1663. African bravery doesn't stand a chance against the Portuguese gunpowder. After her death, the Portuguese had access to expand their slave trade.

Usman Dan Fodio

Shaihu Usman Dan Fodio was a preacher, writer, Sultan of Sokoto, and an Islamic reformer. He was an hausa fulani living in present-day Northern Nigeria. He was known as an Islamic revivalist who lived in the city-state of Gobir. Usman did not encourage the education of women in the religious matter, but that several of his daughters are scholars and writers, with Princess Nana Asmau being the most prominent one.

In his own right, Dan Fodio is a revered religious thinker. He studied classical Islamic science, theology, and philosophy. Dan Fodio, using his influence, sought approval to create a religious model town in Dagel, which was his hometown. Following his teacher Jibri ibn 'Umar argument that it was the duty and power of religious movement to create the ideal society that is free from oppression and any form of vice.

Dan Fodio became the reigning Commander of the Fulani empire, which was then the largest state in Africa after the fulani Holy War. Already vast in Islamic law, he worked to establish an efficient system of government grounded in Islamic law as well. By the time of the war, Usman was already advanced in age, so he retired and handed command to his son Muhammad Bello who is the Sultan of Sokoto.

Uprising of Dan Fodio inspires these Western Jihadis to follow the same: those of Massina Empire founder Seku Amadu, Toucouleur Empire founder El Hadj Umar Tall (who married one of dan Fodio's granddaughters), Wassoulou Empire founder Samori, and Adamawa Emirate founder Modibo Adama, who served as one of dan Fodio's provincial chiefs.

Chapter 7
Creation myths and legends from Africa

How Things Came to Be

There exist many myths that explain how the world came into existence. The Dogon say that twin pairs of creator spirits or gods called Nummo hatched from a cosmic egg. Other groups also speak of the universe, beginning with an egg. People in both southern and northern Africa believed that the world was formed from the body of an enormous snake, sometimes said to span the sky as a rainbow.

The Fon people of Benin tell of Gu, the oldest son of the creator twins Mawu (moon) and Lisa (sun). In the form of an iron sword, Gu came to earth and then became a blacksmith. He was tasked with one thing, and that was to prepare the world for people. He taught humans how to make tools, which in turn enabled them to grow food and build shelters. The San Bushmen of the south say that creation was the work of a spirit named Dxui, who was alternately a man and many other things, such as a flower, a bird, or a lizard.

African Bushmen creation myths

People living on the earth today were not always like that. There was a time when animals and humans lived peacefully underneath the earth with the Kaang, who is considered the Great Master and Lord of all existence. Humans and animals coexisting underneath the earth understood each other. No one suffered any lack. There was light everywhere, even though there's no existence of a sun. It was during this time of perfect happiness that the Kaang began planning how he wanted life above the surface to look like.

Kaang went about the creation of wonders of the world above by first creating wondrous trees whose branches stretched across the entire country. So, he dug a huge hole at the base of the wondrous tree reaching all the way down to the world below the surface where humans and animals lived. He led the first man up when he was done furnishing the world above.

After the first man was taken topside, the first woman came along also through the hole. Then every other person followed suit in coming through the hole. Kaang began helping the animals through. Some of the animals even dug their way through the tree, racing to the top. Soon, the surface was filled with people and animals totally amazed at the new world.

Kaang then gathered everyone together and began to admonish them to live peacefully with one another. He instructed the men and women not to build a fire in this new world or risk evil befallen them. They all agreed in unison, so Kaang left them and went to a secret place where he could watch the world he had created.

The people and animals soon began to enjoy the sun and the feel it had on their skin. When it was night, and the sun disappeared, darkness fell upon the people, and they were greatly distressed. They were cold and couldn't see each other like the animals do in the dark. Someone among them suggested that they built a fire that will give them light and keep everyone warm. This they did, ignoring the warnings of Kaang. As soon as the fire was built, all the animals, out of fear and mistrust for the humans, ran to the mountains and cave.

The people's disobedience came at the cost of them losing their relationship with the animals because they could no longer understand the animals or communicate with them. The seat of trust had now become that of fear between the humans and the animals.

The Bushmen of Africa believes that rain, wind, and thunder have an element of life in them just as plant and animals do. They are of the belief that the human eyes only see the external or body form and that inside the body is a spirit that is alive. That this spirit can move from one person: from a woman to a leopard or from a man to a lion. This is equally the reason why animals exist in the Bushmen of Africa myths.

The Yoruba of Nigeria

All that existed from the beginning was water, land, and sky, and Olorun, who was the ruler of the sky and the creator of the sun, was in charge of things. So, Obatala, a firm believer that the world needed more and who was equally a god, went to Olorun to ask for permission to create lands for all living things to exist. After being granted permission by Olorun, Obatala paid Olorun's first son Orunmila who is also the God of Prophecy, a visit to inform him of his intentions of creating the earth. For his mission to be a success, Orunmila told him to obtain items like a gold chain that would enable him to reach to the water below, a snail's shell filled with sand, palm nuts, a hen, and a black cat, all of which he was to carry in a bag. Obatala set out on his mission first by hanging the gold chain in the sky, then using it as a ladder to climb down. He could only go as far as the length of the gold chain is. Obatala dumped the sand from the snail's shell on the earth with the hen he was carrying. The hen scratches on the sand spreading it around to form the first solid land on earth.

Letting go of the chain, Obatala landed on the earth and called the place of his landing "Ife". He planted the palm nut he came down with, which sprout up to be a palm tree. The cat kept him company while he began to create figures like himself with clay since he was lonely. While still creating, he decided he needed a drink and, as such, made wine out of the juice of the palm tree. While still working, he drank until he was drunk, and the image he created became deformed. Olorun breathed life into the deformed figures, and they turned into human beings. Realizing that his drunkenness had led to the deformity of his creature, he vowed to be the protector of those born deformed. The first Yoruba village at Ife was formed by the first human created by Obatala. Thereafter, Obatala returned to the sky, splitting his time between the sky and Ife.

Olokun, who is the ruler of the sea, was not pleased with Obatala because he never sought her approval before creating land. So, she sent flooding to Obatala's village, Ife, which destroyed half of Obatala's kingdom. The remaining survivors sent Eshu, the messenger of the gods to Obatala and Olorun, asking for help. In response to their plea, Orumila went to earth, causing the water to retreat.

Olokun still was not satisfied, so she challenged Olorun to a weaving contest knowing that he was not a good weaver. Olorun accepted the challenge and sent in a chameleon instead of who mimicked all of Olokun's fabric; Olokun accepted defeat when she saw that she could not win.

The above creation myth originated from the Yoruba people of Nigeria. Ancient Yoruba people were more likely to relate with their city-state than with the Yoruba people as a whole. This is equally the reason why the Yoruba people often quarreled with nearby city-states.

The Yoruba people considered Ife to be very sacred since it was their principal city. This creation myth tried to explain the origin of the Yoruba's sacred city Ife and the creation of humanity.

Bumba Creation

Bumba is the creator of the sky, the sun, and the moon. He created human beings when he was done creating the African cosmogony. The African Cosmogony beings created one another and are not more important than the human beings that came after them. Also, Bumba's three sons followed in their father's footsteps in the creation process. This story also welcomed the support of the Bushongo's nature of communalism. The need for unity for the community and also the earth at large is the major lesson learned from this myth.

The Zimbabweans

This creation myth saw Modimo as the creator of Zimbabwe. He is the custodian of everything good and also had great power to destroy things, bringing natural disasters and devastation in his wake. He was the element of water when he was good and lived in the East. He belonged to the element of fire when he was bad and lived in the west.

Modimo is responsible for the sky, earth, light, root, and he is a rare breed. The first and only of his kind.

The Zulu of Southern Africa

The ancient one Unkulunkulu came from uthlanga or reed and with him came cattle and people. After he was created, he created the earth and all his creatures. The people knew how to make fire and fend for themselves because he taught them. A part of him lives in everything he had created, for he is the beginning of all creation.

The creation Myth of Lower Egypt

The sun god, Ra came out from Nun, a body of water that is so chaotic and was the only thing in existence. Independently, he gave birth to Shu, the god of air, and Tefnut, the goddess of water. Together, they produced the god of earth Geb and Nut, the goddess of the sky. The first humans that existed came out of Ra's tears but were destroyed because of their rebellion. Ra's resentment of the earth caused him to return to the heavens leaving his son Shu to rule the earth. Nut got married to Geb and gave birth to Osiris, Horus, Set, Isis, and Nepthys. Set was a representation of evil, while Osiris represented good. A story exists of Osiris and Set rivalry.

The Berbers of North Africa

A man and a woman unaware of their sex lived together before creation began. They came to the realization that they were different on the day where disagreement ensued between them at the drinking well. The woman's insistence that she must drink first was shoved aside by the man, and the bottom of her clothes was opened on falling to the ground. The now intrigued man inquired about her body, and she said that it represented something good. Eight nights, he stayed with her, and fifty sons and fifty daughters were the product of that eight nights. Surprised by their many children decided to send them above ground who expanded the earth and created mankind.

The Oromo of Ethiopia

By way of a barrier of the stars, the creator Waqa distanced himself from the earth by living in the sky. He is a firm believer in persuasion and trickery. Not so a believer in punishment. He asked his creation man to make a coffin for him, and when it was completed, he tricked and locked them inside the coffin, sending them to the flat earth. The landscape of the earth was formed when he brought a rainstorm that lasted seven years. He released the men from the coffin unharmed, forming women from his blood as soon as the earth was completed. Thirty children were produced to these men who were not pleased with the number of their children. And so, Waqa turned half of the children into animals.

The Akan of Ghana

Nana Nyame, who is the Sky-God, was the main creator. Abrewa lived on earth with her children. They had access to their god through the process of preparing food. Soon, their god was not pleased with this practice anymore, so he moved higher so that there would be a distance between him and Abrewa. Abrewa then asked her kids to build a tower using mortars. Originally, where one mortar was needed to reach their god, she instructed her children to replace the top mortar with one at the bottom resulting in the collapse of the tower and the suffering of her children.

Chapter 8
Influence of other cultures and religions

African culture has greatly been influenced by other cultures, and over the years, the beliefs, customs, and traditions of Africans have been entangled with cultures from other continents. While some people argue that this influence has made positive impacts than negative impacts, others are of the notion that the negative impact of other cultures and religions in the African culture outweighs the positive impact.

Although Africa has diverse cultures gotten from the 54 different countries that are in it, the cultural identity and heritage of most of these countries have been undermined and almost forgotten because of the enormous impact that other cultures and religions have made.

There are terminologies that have been used by different scholars to describe the influence of other cultures and religions on African culture; the ones that are mostly used are civilization and globalization.

Civilization is the imposition of one's standard of culture, beliefs, and traditions on other people, arguably with the intent of achieving a higher standard of behavior while globalization is the idea of interacting and integrating one's culture with other cultures in other to become intertwined.

The earliest form of civilization in Africa started with the influence of the Romans on the Egyptians, which later went further to the Nubia, the Maghreb, and the horn of Africa. Other European countries such as Germany, France, Portugal, and Britain also contributed to the influence made to the African culture. It was said that the French and the Portuguese were able to accept an African as either French or Portuguese if the individual is ready to give up all African culture and adapt their ways of which. After that, they were separated from the rest of the people and defined as the civilized ones.

The Arabs began to invade into North Africa from the middle east in the 7th century A.D, of which. The major influence they made was the Islamization of the North Africans, which later spread to other parts of Africa.

The influence of the South Asians settled in the regions of Kenya, Uganda, South Africa, and Tanzania, and the earliest form of contact that the south Asians had with the Africans goes back to at least 2000 years back; the general migration history of the Asians to Africa was documented from 19th century onward when the number of Asians in East Africa grew from 6,000 to 54,000. The South Asians include the Indians (Hindu), the Muslims, Jains, Sikhs, Goans, and others. This migration brought about economic changes and the influx of other religions, which also influenced the culture of the Africans.

As for the North Americans, their influence started during the 1800s when the western tourist, imperialist, and the explorers began to search out the heart of Africa for natural resources and gemstones, thereby bringing along with them the American culture and Christianity.

The aspects of African culture that has been influenced by other cultures include:

1. Politics

Before the migration of other countries to Africa and the civilization of the Africans; authority, and power of a community is usually bestowed on every member of that community, but as a result of ontology, the power is usually vested to a worthy leader or group of leaders of which their job is to exercise power on behalf of every member of the community and also serve as their representatives in the face of other communities. They are usually known as kings, chiefs, and such other names, depending on the community. These chosen leaders are always dedicated to the growth and well-being of the community, of which there was little or no corruption, coup, or any political riots among them, unlike today.

The influence of the other cultures, predominantly the western culture, led to the abandonment of the African political culture, of which the Democratic culture of politics, which is linked to the westerners, was adopted. This results in African politics being slowly emptied of its quintessence and becoming a game of scandal for various corrupt leaders. The contemporary African politicians no longer see themselves as a representative of the people with the sole mandate of serving them. The leaders today fight, kill, and commit all sorts of atrocities just to step into the position of power. This does not only show that Africans neglected their culture of politics and leadership, but it also shows that whatever political rule that becomes normalized and adopted by the westerners will eventually be normalized and accepted by the Africans, whether it is beneficial or not.

2. Religion

Religion constitutes a very important and intricate part of the African society, and because of this, most of the social, political, and economic activities of the Africans are usually seasoned with religious rites and rituals.

Due to the diversity of the continent, Africa has a lot of religions; although no single religious beliefs and practices can be directly identified as African, there were myths and ritual processes across the geographic and ethnic boundaries that were known to have originated from Africans.

Myths were peculiar to each religion, as discussed earlier in this book, and these serve as the basis of their religion and belief practices. These beliefs, practices, rituals, and religious rites were held in high regard and practiced by every member of each community, but the influence of other cultures has drastically modernized and changed most of these traditional beliefs and practices.

Most present-day Africans are unaware of the religious beliefs and traditional rites practiced by their forefathers. The influence of other cultures has brought in Christianity, and Islamic religion, which is the major and the most practiced religions in Africa today. Some people have ignorantly commented that these religions are part of the indigenous traditional religions in Africa because of the enormous impact that they have made in African society.

The influence of Christian cultures on the African traditional religion was achieved by the Christian missionaries who came from the west, and also, the returned African slaves that were converted to Christians also contributed to the widespread of Christianity in Africa. The Islamic culture began to spread when the Arabs crossed into North Africa from the middle east, of which the North Africans are said to have the highest population of Muslims in Africa.

3. Lifestyle

The influence of other cultures has immeasurably affected the lifestyle of Africans, starting from what they eat to dressing and entertainment. Most of the heritage and culture of the Africa that has to do with lifestyle has been abandoned, and other cultures of the immigrants and colonialist have been adopted. These influenced lifestyles include:

African Dishes: Historically, African countries, like all other countries, are known for some food general to them, and they have also adopted foods from those who migrated from other continents. These traditional African dishes are passed from one generation to the next. It serves as a means of preserving cultural identity, and not only are the traditional dishes being passed down generationally, the adopted dishes that were introduced to the Africans by the immigrant were also being eaten, sold, and the recipes were also transferred to the children.

Some Africans prefer eating dishes belonging to other countries more than their indigenous meals, which show the considerable influence that other cultures have made on the dishes eaten by the Africans. As the world becomes globalized, dishes of different cultures can be assessed by anyone across the globe.

African Clothing: African clothing is the traditional garment worn by the people of Africa. Since Africa is a very big and diverse continent, traditional garment differs throughout each community, some communities are known for wearing dresses with bright colors, some cultures wear embroidered robes, some add attractive beaded necklace and bracelet to their dressing while some employ the use of cowries to adorn their hair, clothes and many more. Unfortunately, these dresses have been replaced by clothing from other cultures, of which western culture being the most adopted dressing of them all.

Western clothing has predominated the dressing of Africans, and traditional wears have been reduced to occasional wears, of which this is also one of the implications of the influence made by other cultures on African culture.

Languages: Just as Africa is blessed with diverse dishes and clothing, Africa also has diverse languages, with more than 2,000 distinct languages, which are one-third of the world's language. Before colonization and before the immigrants came to Africa, the people of Africa are known to communicate in their respective indigenous languages, and the children were able to learn and speak the language fluently. Although there was no general language for the Africans in those days, this did not stop the people from co-existing peacefully.

It was up until people with other cultures from different continents began to migrate to Africa that the need to have a general language to communicate became imminent. Different languages were learned, but the most prominent of them all was the English language.

A vast number of Africans today choose the English language instead of their ancestral language, which gradually leads to the loss of the traditional heritage of their indigenous language. This influence is so great that all sectors in Africa now communicates in English. This influence has made a positive impact on the Africans in that it has broken the communication barrier between communities and countries, and it has also made a negative impact considering the rate at which Africans have adopted the new language and neglected their ancestral languages.

African Music and Entertainment: Music is a natural phenomenon in Africa, ranging from lullabies for infants to the songs of games for children down to the music and dances associated with adulthood.

This music is indigenous to Africa; they speak about the customs, responsibilities, beliefs, values, and rites of the community. They are usually accompanied by dance steps and musical instruments such as traditional drums, rattles, gongs, double bells, harps, djembes, and so on.

This music, dances, and all forms of entertainment done by the Africans in those days have significant meanings and interpretations, but unfortunately, this music has been replaced with English songs. The dancing steps are also on the verge of been forgotten. African musical instruments have been replaced with musical instruments from other cultures such as band-sets, saxophone, Electric drums, etc.

The earliest form of entertainment in Africa was through music, dancing, and playing of different traditional games, traditional plays, and storytelling where the community usually gather together in large groups to enjoy themselves; but now the influence of the western culture has made different means of entertainment available and accessible to everyone in the comfort of their home of which going out and bonding with your loved ones and society is not a criterion to be entertained as it was before the influence of other cultures.

Specific African Practices and beliefs: Due to civilization and influence of other cultures on the African culture, some of Africans religious, traditional practices and beliefs have been completely eroded. Some were good and beneficial practices while others were bad and harmful practices.

An example of harmful practices that was eroded as a result of the influence of other culture was the female genital mutilation which causes a lot of childbearing problems and infections for the young females in West Africa.

An example of the beneficial practices that have ceased among the Africans is the traditional rites for marriage, most cultures in those days follow some steps before conducting any marriage, and this is usually to ensure the safety of their children after leaving their custody. This practice has been neglected and no longer holds among the present time Africans.

4. Education and Technology

The impact of other cultures on African culture is also eminent in the development of the educational system and technological advancement of the continent.

The western influence has tremendously increased the lifestyle of Africans through technology advancement in different areas such as Agriculture, Medicine, Tourist centers, Natural resources, Transport systems, and so on.

Before the influence of other cultures, particularly the Westerners, the only form of education a child gets is the informal education, which is gotten from the parent and the environment around the child. Civilization and the influence of westerners have created a formal Educational system where children can get access to learn different subjects outside his/her family and environment and become useful in life.

Also, premature death and sickness attributed to natural disasters and angry gods were a norm in Africa before the influence of the other cultures. The only form of medicine they had were herbs and plants of which some of them were harmful to the body. Most of the treatments were done by local doctors who have no knowledge about the science of the body. It was after the colonization, independence, and civilization of most African countries that they began to have access to healthcare knowledge and facilities of the westerners, which have greatly reduced the death and disease rate of the Africans.

African sculptures, arts, and crafts have served as a source of income to the continent, agricultural products and natural resources have also been monetized to improve the economy of each country in the continent, and this is a direct result of the influence of other cultures on the African culture.

Apart from the positive impacts of other cultures on the educational and technological advancement highlighted above, the influence of technological advancement and education has also exposed the Africans to cultures that are against their ancestral cultures.

Technological advancement in Africa has been said to promote immorality, violence, profanity among the youths in Africa. Research has shown that many occult practices and gangsterism that occur in some African Tertiary Institutions today are a result of the games, movies, and other technological devices that were introduced to the Africans by the westerners.

In a nutshell, it is obvious that other cultures have left a considerable amount of impact on the African way of life. There have been positive impacts, and there have also been negative impacts. Although no culture is static, all cultures, whether African or not, has experienced change at a certain point or the other, but there are some countries that are conservative about preserving their heritage. An example is aFrench government, which forbids the use of English as the commercial language in the country despite the changes that have occurred in other countries.

In other to avoid the extinction of cultural and traditional values of Africa, there is a need to ensure cultural value rehabilitation in all sectors of the continent and also reduce the influx rate of western influence and other culture's influence on the continent by promoting the indigenous culture.

Although there are few cultures in Africa that still maintained their cultural beliefs and practices, it is said that people without a culture are people with no identity. The culture serves as the unique identity that differentiates people in the world, but now that the world is globalized most cultures have forgotten their identities and adopted the new trending cultures.

Therefore, it is important for any country or continent who wants to preserve their ancestral heritage to curb the rate at which other cultures are influencing their communities.

Chapter 9
Conclusion

Myths are the stories that inform the African people and shape their mode of thinking and actions. Children are usually told certain stories that are believed to have given rise to the cultural norms, values, ideals, principles, mores, and traditions. Throughout African myths, there are stories of men (heroes) who rose to become legends through their actions, which protected or saved the people of their time, such as Bayajida. There are also myths in which animals are the protagonists, such as Anansi.

There are many different countries in Africa, having varied cultural and ethnic groups and languages. The countries in Africa – although independent today – were at a time, colonies of the countries in Europe. Also, during the period of the Trans-Atlantic Slave Trade, many ports in Africa were the locations where slaves were bought and sold. Among those ports were Cairo in Egypt, Lagos in Nigeria, and the Cape in South Africa.

However, before the commencement of the slave trade or even colonization, many foreigners have migrated to African countries for various reasons, one of which is a search for better living conditions. For instance, the Turkish had been migrating to Egypt long before the slave trade began, and as a result, Egypt became an Islamic nation as the Turkish were Muslims. In the case of Nigeria, migrants were usually from other African countries like Ghana, Benin, and Chad. Immigrants into South Africa before the slave trade began were from the Netherlands, France, Great Britain, Germany, Ireland, and Portugal.

Africa was majorly an agricultural continent before the coming of the Europeans. The major occupations were farming and hunting. The materials worn as clothes were usually made of leather, and the only places that were covered were places around the genitals – for both men and women.

Many countries in Africa have different gods (deities), which they believe are the sources of all that exists, and there are over a dozen gods from African nations. The African people worship these deities in one way or another, giving offerings and sacrifices in the hope that these deities will bless them, their families, and their lands.

Africa is a continent that is very rich in culture, and the myths, legends, gods, and goddesses of the various cultural groups are what make the nation great. If you visit a country, specifically a cultural group in Africa, try to familiarize yourself with its people, and you'll be amazed at the many things you will learn.

Made in the USA
Columbia, SC
06 December 2021

50521434R00057